'No desires to move on?'

'I may have desires sometimes, but they aren't always practical.' Kate allowed her gaze to meet his again, and saw that an amused gleam had come into the grey eyes, and at the same instant she realised the implication of what she had just said. To her annoyance she felt the warmth of a blush touch her cheeks. It was unusual for her to react in this way to any man; maybe because he looked so much like Brian she was becoming unnerved by it.

Dear Reader

Although we don't move out of England this month, we do tackle some quite different subjects. In THE STORM AND THE PASSION by Jenny Ashe, Emma has a moral question to face, while Kate in SOMEBODY TO LOVE by Laura MacDonald wonders if she can cope with a short-term affair. In TO DREAM NO MORE by Patricia Robertson, Claire has to overcome fear, while Briony in VET IN POWER by Carol Wood has to overcome the bitterness generated by the feud between her family and Nick's. Problems galore — will our heroines win through?

The Editor

Laura MacDonald lives on the Isle of Wight. She is married and has a grown-up family. She has enjoyed writing fiction since she was a child, but for several years she has worked for members of the medical profession both in pharmacy and in general practice. Her daughter is a nurse and has also helped with the research for Laura's Medical Romances.

Recent titles by the same author:

A CASE OF MAKE-BELIEVE
GYPSY SUMMER

SOMEBODY TO LOVE

BY
LAURA MACDONALD

MILLS & BOON LIMITED
ETON HOUSE   18–24 PARADISE ROAD
RICHMOND   SURREY   TW9 1SR

*First published in Great Britain 1993
by Mills & Boon Limited*

© Laura MacDonald 1993

*Australian copyright 1993
Philippine copyright 1993
This edition 1993*

ISBN 0 263 78188 7

*Set in 10½ on 12½ pt Linotron Times
03-9308-45908*

*Typeset in Great Britain by Centracet, Cambridge
Made and printed in Great Britain*

CHAPTER ONE

IT WAS nearly five o'clock when Kate Riley left the motorway and headed for West Chillerton. It had been a long drive from Lowestoft in Suffolk to her Surrey home town, and she felt hot and tired. But much as she longed for her home she decided she had to call in at the health centre first and see what had been happening while she'd been away at her seminar. Her daughter Nicola was staying with a friend, so she knew she would be all right for another couple of hours, but things at the centre had been a little fraught between the partners and she wondered if the difficulties had been resolved in her absence.

Kate was a psychotherapist and counsellor attached to a busy three-partner GP practice. One of the partners, Ruth Scott, had contracted glandular fever and there had been difficulty in finding a suitable locum in her absence, resulting in a gradual build-up of tension.

She drew up on the forecourt of the centre and parked her elderly Volvo, then with a sigh she stretched and flexed her fingers before climbing out and retrieving her briefcase and handbag from the back seat.

In Reception she called a brief greeting to Julie and Lynn, the two receptionists on duty that afternoon, then headed for her consulting-room on the first floor. Afterwards she was to remember the anxious expressions on the girls' faces, but at the time she wasn't really aware of anything untoward, her only thought being to get herself a cool drink. And it wasn't until she was in her room sorting through the last week's mail and sipping a mineral water that Bernard Rayner, the senior partner, tapped on the door.

'Hello, Kate, may I come in?' he asked.

'Of course, Bernard.' She smiled up at the huge bearded figure — then her smile faded when she saw his serious expression.

'How did your seminar go?' he asked.

'Fine, thanks. . .but is there anything wrong. . .?'

'Kate, you're not to worry, because I'm sure it isn't anything serious, but. . .'

'What isn't?' She stared at him, mildly alarmed now.

'It's Nicola. . .' he began.

Kate's eyes widened at the mention of her daughter's name.

'Nicola! What is it? What's wrong?' she demanded, half rising to her feet. Fear clutched at her heart as she stared at Bernard.

'She's had a bit of an accident. She came off her bike on her way home from school — a slight collision, I believe — a couple of her friends brought her in here.'

'So where is she?' Kate was on her feet by this time and preparing to hurry from her room.

'Steady on, Kate—she's at the hospital at the moment,' he told her, then catching sight of her horrified expression he added hastily, 'She'd hurt her arm and bumped her head, and Tom thought she should have some X-rays, just to be on the safe side. He's taken her down there now in his car.'

Kate stared at him, trying to take in what he had told her, then she sank back into her chair.

'Try not to worry, Kate. It really didn't sound too serious,' said Bernard sympathetically. 'I should think they'd be back soon——'

'Who's Tom?' asked Kate, abruptly interrupting him in mid-sentence.

Bernard frowned, then smiled. 'Of course, you haven't met him yet, have you? He's Ruth's locum, Tom Beresford. He answered our ad the day after you went and he was able to start immediately. He's first-rate, I know you'll like him. . .'

But Kate wasn't listening. She'd grabbed her bag and her car keys from the desk and was heading for the door.

'Where are you going, Kate?' Bernard followed her into the corridor.

'To the hospital.'

'I'll take you. . .'

'No, Bernard, thank you. You have a surgery to do.'

'But you've had a shock. . .maybe one of the girls. . .'

'No, really, I'm fine.'

She drove mechanically to the hospital, the engine

of her Volvo still warm from her long drive, her calm exterior hiding the sick panic that was forming in the pit of her stomach. By the time she arrived, her mind was a teeming mass of emotions while her lips silently formed a prayer for her daughter's safety. Nicola was the most important person in Kate's life, and had been from the moment she'd been born thirteen years before. Kate knew that if anything happened to her daughter the light would go out of her own life. Bernard had said that he didn't think it was serious, but had he just said that to help her stop worrying? Hadn't he also said something about a collision? A collision with what, for heaven's sake? Another bike? A pedestrian or a bus? Kate shuddered.

When she reached Casualty her stomach was churning, and by the time she gave her name at the desk she had convinced herself that the worst had happened. Woodenly she did as she was told and sat down in the waiting area, then only moments later, although to Kate it seemed like hours, the sister on duty called her.

'Mrs Riley? Would you like to come and see your daughter?' As Kate followed her she added, 'Nicola's had her X-rays, she's over here in a cubicle. Dr Beresford is with her. . .is he a relative?'

Kate shook her head. 'I don't even know him.'

As the sister drew back the cubicle curtains Kate's first impression was of two heads close together — the hair of a similar wheat colour. Nicola was lying on the couch and a man was sitting in a chair by her side. They both looked up.

'Mum!' exclaimed Nicola, then catching sight of her mother's expression she sighed and said, 'You can stop worrying. I'm OK, aren't I, Tom?'

Kate stopped in her tracks, her gaze transferring from her daughter to the man at her side. Then her breath caught in her throat as his cool grey eyes met hers. Just for an instant she had thought it was Brian. He was certainly like him, or rather how he had looked when she'd first met him, but Brian would be in his forties now, and the man before her could barely be thirty.

There was silence as she struggled to regain her composure, then as she turned from that cool stare to her daughter again relief swamped over her and she felt her knees go weak. She might have stumbled, but the man had risen to his feet and as if anticipating her reaction had reached out his arm and steadied her. His fingers beneath her elbow were firm, reassuring, then he stood aside so that she could reach the couch.

She took a deep breath. 'Thank you.' Then she moved forward and embraced her daughter. 'Nicola, whatever happened?' Fiercely Kate hugged her, overcome with emotion.

'Oh, nothing much.' Nicola squirmed with embarrassment. 'I collided with a van, that's all, and fell off my bike.'

'A van?' Kate's eyes widened and involuntarily she turned to the man at her side.

'It was only a glancing blow,' he said calmly. 'Nicola's sprained her wrist and has got a nasty bump on her head. We're just waiting for the X-ray results.' He smiled. 'Maybe we should introduce ourselves while we're waiting. I'm Tom Beresford, and I guess you must be Nicola's mum.' He held out his hand, and Kate found hers grasped in a firm handshake.

'Kate Riley,' she replied weakly. 'I gather you're doing locum for Ruth Scott.'

He nodded. 'Yes, and I understand you've been away on a seminar. It's funny how everything happens when you turn your back, isn't it?' He grinned at Nicola as he spoke, and she grinned back.

'You can say that again,' said Kate grimly, then sank thankfully down on to the chair as once again her knees threatened to give way.

A little later a doctor arrived to tell them that Nicola's X-rays showed no signs of a skull fracture, so the extent of her injuries was a sprained left wrist, grazes to her left leg and a lump the size of an egg on her head. As they prepared to leave the casualty unit Kate thanked Tom Beresford for taking care of Nicola.

'Don't mention it. I was glad to be of help,' he replied. 'Now, do you have transport?'

Kate nodded. 'Yes, I have my car.'

'Well, in that case, I'll leave my patient in her mum's capable hands,' he said, winking at Nicola. 'Will I see you tomorrow?' he asked Kate as they stepped outside.

'Yes, I'll be at work in the morning,' she said.

Moments later, after she had settled Nicola comfortably into the passenger seat of the Volvo, a car horn sounded behind her, and as she turned she saw Tom Beresford at the wheel of a navy blue BMW. He raised his hand in farewell and swept from the hospital car park. For a moment before climbing into her own car, Kate watched him, struck once again by his resemblance to Brian, but this time it was not what had attracted her to Nicola's father that she remembered, but the disastrous events that had followed, and she consciously found herself trying to put the new locum out of her mind.

This, however, proved to be more difficult than she thought, for her daughter seemed to have been quite smitten by the attentions of the handsome young doctor and didn't want to appear to talk about anything else.

'He's been working in America,' she told Kate as they drove to the converted mews cottage in the heart of town where they had lived for the past five years. 'He said he's been working on research for a large pharmaceutical firm in Boston,' she added importantly.

'So what's he doing as Dr Scott's locum?' asked Kate, faintly irritated at the attention Tom Beresford seemed to be receiving from her daughter.

'He's been here for six months, visiting his family. He saw the advert and decided to apply because he was getting bored.' Nicola sighed. 'Wasn't it kind of him to take me to the hospital?'

'Very,' admitted Kate. 'You were privileged. Patients don't usually get that sort of treatment. If they're not an ambulance case they have to make their own way to Casualty.'

'Tom said it was the least he could do, especially as you weren't around to do it for me.'

Kate threw her daughter a sharp look, but she appeared to be gazing out of the window. As they climbed from the car a little later she said, 'I'm not sure you should be calling Dr Beresford by his Christian name.'

'He asked me to,' explained Nicola, tossing back her tousled hair. Kate frowned as they made their way between tubs bright with busy lizzie and lobelia, then she unlocked the door to their cottage.

They spent a quiet evening after eating the light supper which Kate prepared. Nicola didn't seem particularly interested in what Kate had done at her seminar, and when Kate tried to find out what her daughter had been doing while she'd been away, she seemed evasive.

'Would you like to go shopping on Saturday?' asked Kate as they finished their meal.

Nicola shrugged. 'I don't know. I may be seeing some friends.'

'You mean Beverley?'

'No, not Beverley, some other friends.'

Kate frowned. Beverley was Nicola's best friend and it was unusual for her to be seeing someone else, for as a rule the two girls spent all their free time together. 'I hope you two haven't fallen out while you've been staying together,' she remarked.

'Of course we haven't — don't be silly!'

Kate knew better than to try to pursue the matter further, but when she would have changed the subject, Nicola suddenly mentioned Tom Beresford again.

'Did you know that Tom goes motor racing?' she asked.

'How could I know?' Kate laughed. 'I hadn't even met him before today. You know much more about him than I do.' She glanced up at the kitchen clock. 'Now what would you like to do?'

'I'm going to watch a video,' said Nicola and, taking an apple from a bowl of fruit on the table, she bit into it and ambled off to her room.

Kate was vaguely relieved. She had been quite prepared to spend some time with her daughter that evening, especially in view of the fact that they had been apart for the last week and now because of her accident, but at the same time she had a lot of work to catch up on.

She went upstairs to the corner of her bedroom that she used as her study and began checking her schedule for the next week, but as she worked, her mind constantly wandered, and in the end she threw down her pen in exasperation and rubbed her eyes. Maybe she was just tired after her long drive and the trauma that had been waiting for her at the end. She sighed, looping her smooth ash-blonde hair back behind her ears, and attempted to concentrate once again.

Outside in the street a car accelerated noisily away. Motor racing. Nicola had said Tom Beresford went motor racing. So what if he did? What did it matter to her? Why did Tom Beresford keep coming into her mind?

She sighed again, then stood up and walked to the window. She knew she really shouldn't need to ask herself that question because deep down she knew the answer. Her meeting with the locum had disturbed her for one reason—because he so strongly resembled her ex-husband. Seeing him with Nicola had unnerved her, because she had always felt that Nicola resembled her father, but the disturbing part was that there seemed to have been some uncanny rapport between Tom Beresford and her daughter.

Outside, the mews yard was a riot of summer colours from the flower-packed tubs and window-boxes, but Kate hardly noticed as her mind travelled reluctantly back to how it had once been.

She had met Brian Riley in her nursing days, and she had fallen for him the moment she set eyes on him. He had been an ambulance driver attached to the same hospital, a little older than her but very attractive, and furthermore, he had seemed to feel the same way about her as she did about him. Within a month of meeting they were sharing a flat, and when Kate found she was pregnant they made plans to marry.

The marriage began to go wrong almost from the

moment that Nicola was born and Kate had found out that one woman wasn't sufficient to satisfy Brian Riley's fragile ego. The first year of Nicola's life was the worst year that Kate could ever remember. Her relationship with her husband deteriorated to the point where he began physically taking out his frustrations on her when she demanded that he give up his extra-marital activities.

They had separated soon afterwards, and Kate had filed for divorce on the grounds of Brian's adultery and his unreasonable conduct. She had eventually been awarded custody of Nicola, and with the help of her sister Fran had begun to rebuild her career. Brian had since remarried and had emigrated to New Zealand, but the whole episode had left Kate emotionally devastated.

When a colleague had suggested she seek help in the form of counselling she had indignantly refused, unable to accept that she could be in need of such a thing, but as time passed and she seemed no nearer to recovering from the emotional scars that Brian had inflicted, she eventually recognised her need for help. Initially she went for counselling, which had led to a further year of psychotherapy, from which she had emerged confident and in control of her own life once more, although she still remained wary of long-term relationships.

After her term of therapy Kate had gone on to qualify as a health visitor, and it had been during this period of her life that she had fully come to realise the vast numbers of people who would benefit from various forms of counselling. Partly through this and partly because of her own experiences she had begun her own training as a psychotherapist, and when she had qualified she had applied for the position attached to the group practice in West Chillerton. When she was told she had the job she and Nicola had moved into the attractive little mews cottage where they had lived quite happily for the past five years.

Now, at thirty-eight, Kate was more contented than at any other time in her life. Nicola was the most important thing in her world, with her work coming second, and the fact that there was no man in her life didn't unduly worry her.

There had been a couple of light relationships since Brian, but that was all they had been, and she had gradually forgotten just how much Brian had once meant to her and just how much he had hurt her. Until today, when she had looked into Tom Beresford's cool gaze and been transported into the past, back to the moment when she had first met Brian and experienced a desire she'd never known before.

It was ridiculous really, she told herself as she finally abandoned all thoughts of work and prepared for bed. From her training she should have known that this sort of thing was quite common — a stranger evoking forgotten sensations — but somehow when it happened it was never quite as the text-books described it. If she was really honest with herself she was faintly irritated that Bernard Rayner and his partners had employed Tom Beresford and not the other, older man who had applied for the position.

She knew her feelings were quite irrational, that Tom Beresford was no doubt more than suitable for the post, but Kate just felt she would feel safer if he wasn't around.

Before going to bed she looked in on Nicola and found her daughter fast asleep, her arms around her cuddly pink hippo and her television still on.

Kate switched off the set, gently covered the sleeping girl with her duvet and for a moment stood looking down at her. She looked vulnerable in sleep and very young, almost like a small child again, the lashes dark against the smooth downy cheek, and Kate felt her breath catch in her throat. She could have been killed today. . .if that van had been inches closer. . .if she'd fractured her skull when she'd fallen. . .while she, her mother, had been miles away, working. If she'd been around maybe it wouldn't have happened. Kate sighed, logic telling her that was ridiculous. It would have happened wherever she'd been, but how often in the past had she had these battles with her conscience? How often had she been torn between her work and her duty to her daughter? But she had to work if she was to provide a home for them both, and the quality of their lives was important to Kate. Ever since Brian had gone Kate had been determined that Nicola shouldn't suffer and that she would endeavour to be both mother and father to the girl.

Later, as Kate brushed her hair, she told herself

that her troubled thoughts that evening and her inability to work were a direct result of Nicola's accident and coping with the resulting emotion over what might have happened, but deep inside she knew that was only partly the case. Tom Beresford's resemblance to Brian had been almost as disturbing as Nicola's reaction to him.

Her last thought before she went to sleep was the comforting one that at least there would be no need for her daughter to come into contact with the locum again even if she, Kate, was forced to work in close proximity to him.

CHAPTER TWO

THE following morning Kate persuaded Nicola to take the day off school.

'Oh, Mum, for goodness' sake, there's no need for that!' Her daughter sighed as she poured herself a glass of fresh orange juice.

'Well, I think there is,' said Kate firmly. 'Your arm is swollen, and that was a nasty bang on your head. I think you should stay quietly here today.'

'What, on my own? Great fun that'll be!'

'Just for today, Nicky, then after the weekend I'm sure you'll be all right for school.' Kate was aware that her voice had taken on a pleading tone. She paused, then seeing the rebellious look on her daughter's face she said, 'I'll pop back later and have a bit of lunch with you, and Lottie will be in soon, so you'll have someone around for a couple of hours at least.'

'Big deal!' Nicola hunched her shoulders, but Kate knew that her daughter got on well with Lottie Downer who came in twice a week to clean the cottage. There had been several occasions in the past when Lottie had acted as child-minder when Nicola had been ill and too young to leave on her own.

'Maybe Beverley will come over after school,' said

Kate hopefully, but Nicola didn't answer, leading Kate to wonder again if there had been some sort of rift between the girls. When she was nearly ready for work the phone rang, and as Kate answered it, she recognised her sister Fran's voice.

'So you're back, then,' said Fran. 'How was Lowestoft?'

'Fine, thanks. But it's good to be home. Everything all right with you?'

'Yes not too bad. Ron's hurt his back again — too much gardening. Is Nicky OK?'

'Yes — well, not really.' Kate went on to briefly explain about Nicola's accident.

'Oh, Kate!' her sister sounded concerned. 'You should have rung me.'

'There wasn't anything you could do, honestly, Fran.'

'So how is she today?' Fran didn't sound convinced.

'She's much better, but I've insisted she stays at home,' said Kate, catching her daughter's eye across the table and pulling a face at her.

'Oh dear, she could have come over here, but I have to go in to Guildford. . .'

'Don't worry, Fran, she'll be all right, really. Look, I'm afraid I must dash, or I'll be late for work.'

'Yes, all right, Kate — but listen, I'll ring you tonight and maybe we can arrange something for the weekend. Perhaps you and Nicola can come over. . .'

'OK, Fran, fine. Bye now.' Kate hung up and looked at Nicola just as the kitchen door opened from the yard and Lottie called out.

'Auntie Fran said something about going over to them this weekend,' Kate said quickly, and was pleased to see her daughter's eyes briefly light up. She knew she liked spending time with her cousins in their large rambling old house that backed on to the Thames. Struggling into the blue jacket of her linen suit, she glanced up as Lottie appeared in the doorway. Lottie was a widow in her late fifties, a tall thin lady, somewhat eccentric, who always wore a fluffy blue hat, even when she was working.

'Hello, Lottie. Could you just do the usual today, please?' said Kate. 'Oh, and Nicola will be staying home from school.'

'Why? Is she ill?' The older woman was buttoning her pink nylon overall, but she paused and looked suspiciously at Nicola.

'Not really, but I'll leave her to tell you all about it,' said Kate with a frantic look at the clock.

'Just a minute, Mrs Riley,' said Lottie. 'Is Dr Scott at the centre today?'

'No, she's on sick leave at the moment,' explained Kate. 'Why, did you want to see her?'

Lottie sniffed. 'Yes, I did, as a matter of fact.' She said it in a way that implied that Dr Scott had no right to take time off.

'Well, she has a locum who will be seeing her patients while she's away,' said Kate, her gaze flickering to Nicola as she spoke.

'Is it a man?' Lottie looked suspicious.

'Yes.'

'I'm not seeing no man!'

'But he's lovely,' said Nicola suddenly. 'I had to see him yesterday. Honestly, Lottie, he's not a bit like a doctor.'

'Nicola!' exclaimed Kate half disapprovingly.

'Well, he isn't. Let's face it, he's not a bit like Dr Rayner or Dr Symonds, is he?' Nicola turned to Lottie. 'His name's Tom and he's been working in America.'

'I don't like Americans,' said Lottie gloomily.

Kate fled, leaving Nicola and Lottie to chat amiably together.

At the health centre Kate spent the first half-hour in her consulting room on the first floor going through the mail which she had abandoned the previous day and trying to organise her schedule for the coming week. She had two aspects of her work to consider; counselling and psychotherapy. Clients she saw for counselling were quite often on an emergency basis when some crisis had occurred and they needed to talk things over with a professional in order to help them to find a fairly speedy solution to their problem.

Appointments for clients receiving psychotherapy, on the other hand, could be spread over a much longer period of time, sometimes even months or years, in extreme cases on a daily basis, as she helped them to go deeply into their past experiences to recognise the cause of their present problems.

Most of her clients were referred from the GPs by whom Kate was employed, but occasionally she was approached by people not registered with the practice who had heard of her methods and hoped she might be able to help them. Sometimes the procedure worked in reverse, and during therapy Kate would recognise a medical problem and refer the client to the GP.

She cleared her desk and glancing at her appointment book saw that her first client of the morning was Joe, a young man of twenty who had been attending therapy for about three months after losing his job, then being ordered out of his home by his stepfather. She pressed her intercom and asked Julie in Reception if she would please send Joe up to her room, then while she was waiting for him, she stood up and strolled to the window.

Her room overlooked the centre's private car park, which was surrounded by flower-beds. Kate was just thinking how splendid the roses were that year and was about to turn away when a dark blue car pulled into the car park and stopped beneath her window. She paused, then stepping to the side of the window she peered down to watch as the occupant of the car got out.

It was a very warm morning, and Tom Beresford was dressed in an open-necked shirt and loose-fitting khaki-coloured trousers. The cuffs of his shirt were turned casually back, a tie loosely knotted at the neck, the overall effect managing to appear very American. His short, wheat-coloured hair gleamed in the morning sunlight, and just for a moment, as he opened the rear door of his car and pulled out his case, a bundle of papers, and his jacket, Kate was aware of the ripple of muscles beneath the cotton shirt. Once again she was forcibly struck by how like Brian he was.

Then, as if he knew she was there, he glanced up.

She caught her breath and quickly stepped backwards. The last thing she wanted was for him to think that she had been watching him.

She had no more time then, however, to give the locum another thought as Joe arrived for his fifty-minute session. In spite of the warmth of the day Joe was huddled into a worn, navy blue duffel coat a couple of sizes too small for him. The sleeves barely covered his thin white wrists, and even though Kate offered to turn on her heater he refused to take the coat off. Eventually she managed to bring the conversation back to the point at which they had stopped in the previous session, where Joe had been talking of his childhood and his early relationship with his mother.

Kate knew there wasn't going to be any quick or easy solution for Joe's problems, which were deep-rooted and would require many more months of careful listening and allowing him to talk.

When Joe had gone after Kate had arranged his next appointment, Julie rang through to ask Kate if she would see a young girl who was a patient of

Ruth Scott and who had just been told she was pregnant. The girl was very distressed and required urgent counselling, so Kate agreed to see her before her next client. The girl was silent and unco-operative, so all that Kate was really able to do was to talk through the various options open to her, but at least by the time she left Kate's room, the girl was aware that she did have options.

As she watched her leave, Kate sighed and removed the glasses she wore for close work. The girl hadn't been very much older than Nicola, she too had come from a one-parent family, and Kate found herself wondering what problems she would have to face in the future with her own daughter. That there would be problems she had no doubt. She was not complacent enough to imagine that being a psychotherapist exempted her from life's trials, but she could only hope that, when they came, she would recognise them and know how to deal with them.

She saw one more client before meeting the partners for coffee and discussion in the staff-room. This client was a man in his late fifties who was in the early stages of emphysema but who had found it impossible to give up smoking because of the press-ures in his life. Kate was allowing him to talk through these pressures so that with luck it would become obvious to him in which areas he could let go and introduce more relaxation into his life.

When Kate finally made her way to the staff-room

it was to find that the doctors had finished their surgeries and were already there.

'Ah, here she is now,' said Bernard. 'Let me pour you a coffee, Kate, you look as if you've had a tough morning.' He turned away to the coffee machine, and Kate glanced round the room. Malcolm Symonds was on the telephone and Tom Beresford was lounging in an armchair, his legs crossed, a cup and saucer in one hand; his gaze met Kate's.

'Have you?' he asked quietly.

'Have I what?' she frowned.

'Had a tough morning?'

She shrugged slightly, then took her coffee from Bernard. 'It's always a bit difficult getting back into the swing of things after being away, but no, it wasn't that bad really.'

'So how was Lowestoft?' asked Bernard as Kate sat down. 'I didn't have the chance to ask you yesterday.'

'It was very good. It dealt more with analysis than with therapy, but it gave much food for thought.'

'How did it go with Ted this morning?' asked Malcolm Symonds as he finished his telephone conversation and replaced the receiver. 'His results from his last bronchoscopy weren't good, he really needs to stop smoking now.'

'I think we're getting somewhere at last,' said Kate. 'At least he doesn't see me as an enemy now, which I suppose is something.'

'Did you see Ruth's patient?' asked Tom suddenly. 'The little girl with the positive pregnancy test?'

'I did,' replied Kate. 'She didn't say much, but I've persuaded her to come in tomorrow, but with her mother this time.'

'I got the impression there's not a lot of support from her mother, complete uninterest in fact,' observed Tom.

'Well, we'll see' said Kate, sipping her coffee.

'By the way,' he said smoothly, 'how is your daughter after her mishap yesterday?'

Kate looked up sharply. Had Tom Beresford intended criticism by linking his enquiry about Nicola with the girl they had just been discussing? But there was nothing about his demeanour that suggested that; in fact there appeared genuine concern in the grey eyes as he waited for her reply, and she came to the conclusion that she was being unnecessarily touchy where he was concerned.

'Nicola's fine,' she said. 'And thank you again for what you did. I persuaded her to take a day off school just to be on the safe side, but she wasn't keen.'

'You should think yourself lucky,' said Malcolm with a sigh. 'We've just found out that Theo's been playing truant. He hates school.'

'Well, at least that's one problem I don't have with Nicola,' said Kate. 'She seems to love school.'

'She told me her father lives in New Zealand,' said Tom as he drained his cup and stood up.

'That's right, he does.' Once again Kate allowed

her gaze to meet his and she found herself wondering just what else her daughter had told this man about their private lives.

After that they went their separate ways, the three doctors to take the morning's house calls and Kate to return to her room for the final therapy session of the morning. This time it concerned a woman in her thirties, Stephanie, who had left her husband and two children for another man only to find that that relationship was now floundering. Kate was helping her to understand that the difficulties she was now experiencing were very similar to the initial ones she had had with her husband.

As the session drew to a close and Stephanie left in tears, as she usually did after a painful bout of self-analysis, Kate decided she would keep her promise to Nicola and go home for lunch. Picking up her bag and car keys, she left her room and ran lightly down the stairs. She hurried through reception, and was about to push open the large double doors when she heard voices that she recognised, and she stopped and turned in surprise.

Half hidden by a large cheese plant in the waiting area of Reception, Nicola was deep in conversation with Tom Beresford.

Slowly Kate walked towards them, and as her daughter looked up and saw her, Kate noticed she was wearing make-up.

'What are you doing here?' she asked. 'You're supposed to be at home resting.'

'I came to meet you.' Her daughter's reply was defensive, almost challenging.

Tom Beresford glanced from mother to daughter. 'And I was just catching up on my patients's progress,' he said lightly. 'Making sure there are no ill effects.'

'Well, now you're here, we might as well have a sandwich in the staff-room instead of going all the way home again,' said Kate to Nicola.

'I have a better idea,' said Tom. 'Why don't I take you both to lunch at that nice little place in the precinct?'

'Oh, great, you mean Traddles?' Nicola's eyes lit up and she tossed back her fair tousled hair. To Kate's dismay her daughter at that moment looked at least sixteen.

'Oh, we couldn't possibly impose. . .' began Kate.

'Nonsense, you won't be imposing. I'll be glad of the company,' said Tom. 'Hold on a moment, I'll just get my jacket.'

Moments later they were walking through the busy shopping precinct, and when they reached the trendy new restaurant Tom found them a table on a raised dais that overlooked the main shopping area.

They all ordered jacket potatoes with different fillings, then as they waited for the food to arrive Nicola asked Tom what part of America he had been working in.

Kate was aware of a vague uneasiness at her daughter's apparent forwardness where the locum was concerned, but he seemed not to mind in the least.

'I was living in Boston, Massachusetts,' he told her. 'It's a fantastic place. The company I worked for was right in the centre of Boston, but the apartment I rented was on the outskirts, overlooking a park. I was lucky to be there in October and saw it in the fall—an experience not to be missed. Have you been to the States?' He half turned towards Kate.

She shook her head. 'I'm afraid not—Nicola would like to go, but our holidays have all been Continental or local ones.' She didn't add that their budget would never have run to a holiday in the States. Life had been enough of a struggle as it was without expense like that.

'Have you been to Disneyland?' asked Nicola, putting her elbows on the table, resting her chin on her hands and gazing at Tom.

'Not Disneyland, but I have been to Disney World in Florida,' he said. 'I went with one of the guys I was working with and his children.'

'Absolutely all my friends have been.' Nicola gave a huge sigh.

'Well, maybe you will one day,' said Tom sympathetically, then glanced up as the waitress arrived with their food. They remained silent as she put the plates down, then as she moved away Tom picked up his knife and fork and said, 'I loved the States so much that I plan to go back there.'

His gaze met Kate's as he spoke, and for some

reason which she couldn't explain she was forced to look away.

'When will you go?' asked Nicola, looking momentarily dismayed, then seconds later enthusiastically tucking into her potato.

'Probably after this locum job. I need to sort out work permits and visas, but it's all practically settled.'

'Will you do research again?' asked Kate.

He shook his head. 'No, I've been offered a post in general practice.'

'In Boston?' Suddenly she was curious and wanted to know more.

'No, not in Boston. In Philadelphia, Pennsylvania. It'll be a challenge, and I shall enjoy that. I'm not very good at staying in the same place for too long. How about you?'

'Me?' Kate looked startled for a moment.

'Yes, have you been here in West Chillerton for long?'

'About five years.'

'No desires to move on?'

'I may have desires sometimes, but they aren't always practical.' Kate allowed her gaze to meet his again and saw that an amused gleam had come into the grey eyes, and at the same instant she realised the implication of what she had just said. To her annoyance she felt the warmth of a blush touch her cheeks. It was unusual for her to react in this way to any man, and she could only put it down to the fact that because Tom looked so much like Brian she was becoming unnerved by it. She was aware that his gaze had moved and he seemed to be taking in her appearance — the cornflower-blue linen suit and crisp white shirt, her smooth ash-blonde hair drawn back from her face and fastened at the nape of her neck with a black bow, and finally her eyes, which were almost the exact blue of her suit.

The answering response in his own eyes to what he saw was only too obvious, but Kate was saved from further embarrassment by Nicola, who had apparently mercifully remained oblivious to the body language between the adults.

'Will you go motor racing in Philadelphia, Tom?' she asked.

'Oh, I don't know about that. I tend to watch these days rather than take part.'

'I think it's exciting,' said Nicola. 'I always watch it on the television.'

'I didn't know you liked motor racing.' Kate stared at her daughter.

'I expect there are a lot of things about me you don't know,' Nicola shrugged, and pushed her plate away.

Kate opened her mouth to make some retort, but Tom quickly intervened. 'Tell you what, perhaps you'd like to come to watch some Formula One racing with me one weekend.' He looked from one to the other of them. Nicola's face lit up at his suggestion, but Kate's expression was doubtful.

'Both of you,' he went on firmly.

'Thank you, Tom, that would be great,' said Nicola with a haughty look at her mother.

As they were finishing their lunch a group of young people came into the restaurant. One of the girls glanced in their direction, then when she saw Nicola, detached herself from the others and came across. She was a striking-looking girl with a creamy complexion. She was dressed entirely in black, and her red hair was plaited and woven about her face with beads and thin pieces of coloured cord.

'Hi, Nick,' she said, ignoring Kate and Tom. 'Where've you been?'

'I had a bit of an accident,' Nicola told her. 'But I'll be back on Monday.'

Kate glanced at her daughter and noticed that she looked uncomfortable. She looked at the girl again. She was a stranger to Kate, as were the other members of the group, and as she moved away to join them again Kate asked, 'Who was that, Nicky?'

'Her name's Kim.'

'I haven't seen her before, have I?'

'No, she's fairly new at school.'

As the girl Kim joined the group and they moved away, one or two of them looked back at Nicola and one of the boys shouted out something, but Kate didn't catch what he said. Before she had the chance to say anything else, Tom looked at his watch and stood up.

'I have to be going,' he said. 'I have one more house call to make over at Parkfield before afternoon surgery.'

'Good, you can give me a lift home,' said Nicola.

'Nicola. . .!' Kate began, but Tom only grinned good naturedly.

'OK, come on, let's go and get my car.'

The vague feeling of unease persisted through the afternoon. Kate tried hard to put it out of her mind as she saw a client for bereavement counselling, but it was back later when she conducted a group therapy session for clients with alcohol-related problems, then at the end of the afternoon, as she was tidying her desk, there came a knock at her door.

'Come in,' she called, and when she glanced up, she wasn't really surprised when Tom Beresford put his head round the door. It was almost as if she'd expected him to come and see her, as if she'd been waiting for him all afternoon, as if there had been some unfinished business between them.

But that was ridiculous, she told herself, for apart from the fact that he had been kind to her daughter and had bought them both lunch, there was nothing about the new locum that made him any different from any other man she came into contact with.

Except that he reminded her of her ex-husband, of course, and Kate already knew she had to put that out of her mind as quickly as possible.

'So this is the inner sanctum,' he said, glancing round her consulting-room, then, coming right into the room, he added, 'This is where people reveal their innermost thoughts and secrets.'

Kate frowned, immediately on the defensive at what she thought was a sceptical note in his voice.

'You sound as if you don't approve of psycho-therapy,' she remarked.

'I wouldn't go that far,' he smiled. 'It has its place. . .but I didn't come here to discuss the ethics of psychodynamics. I came to see if you'd have dinner with me tomorrow night.'

CHAPTER THREE

KATE stared at him, not sure what to say; surprised by his request and yet not surprised. It was almost as if it was inevitable that he should ask her out, a natural progression from the moment they first looked at each other.

She swallowed as he waited for her answer. 'I'm not really sure about tomorrow night,' she hedged at last.

'Is there a problem?' he asked.

'Only that I may be going over to my sister's with Nicola for the weekend.'

'Only may be?' He raised one eyebrow, and Kate felt a fluttering inside.

Quickly she looked away. It had been a long time since she'd felt anything remotely like that, and she wasn't sure she remembered how to cope with it.

'I had thought about taking Nicola over and letting her stay there as I have a lot of jobs to catch up on, but on the other hand, I expect my sister will talk me into staying,' she explained.

'Tell you what,' Tom said easily, 'I'll give you a ring around lunchtime tomorrow—by then you should know what's happening.'

'All right.' She found herself nodding and agreeing with him when she knew she should be making it quite plain that she didn't want anything other than a professional relationship.

He raised his hand in farewell, and helplessly she watched him leave.

On her way home she tried to suppress the feelings of excitement he had aroused, telling herself firmly that she was only attracted to him because he reminded her of Brian and of how it had once been between them before things had gone wrong. She had made up her mind years ago that she didn't want another heavy relationship — and besides, she reasoned with herself as she drove into her garage, Tom Beresford was too young for her. Then as she fitted her key into the lock of her front door she found herself smiling. She had allowed herself to become carried away by her speculations when all the poor man had done was to ask her out for a meal!

Nicola was sitting on the stairs in conversation with someone on the telephone. Kate dumped a carrier full of shopping that she'd collected from the supermarket, kicked off her shoes and filled the kettle. She was just popping two teabags into the teapot when Nicola appeared in the kitchen doorway.

'Hello, are you feeling better?' asked Kate.

'I wasn't feeling ill,' said Nicola.

'Maybe I'd better re-phrase that. How is your arm and the lump on your head?'

'OK.' Nicola lifted her hair so that Kate could see the purplish bruise on the side of her head. Her left arm also looked less swollen than it had the night before. 'Why were you smiling?' asked Nicola suddenly.

'When?' Kate paused and looked up.

'When you came through the front door just now. You were smiling.'

'Was I?' Kate reflected over what she had been smiling at, then she hesitated. Suddenly she realised she didn't want to tell her daughter that Tom Beresford had asked her out. She wasn't sure why, but somehow she imagined it would cause a reaction from Nicola. It wasn't worth it, especially as she had decided that she wasn't going. Kate was fairly surprised by the realisation. When had she decided? And why? She wasn't sure, but the sensible side of her nature told her that it was for the best. In spite of that, she still shied away from telling her daughter. Instead she tried to steer the conversation away from why she had been smiling when she came through the front door.

'Who was that on the phone?' she asked casually as she perched on one of the kitchen stools, and curling her hands around her mug, she sipped her tea.

'Beverley,' said Nicola briefly.

Kate looked up quickly, pleased that it had been Beverley and hopeful that her fears had been incorrect and that the two girls hadn't fallen out after all. They'd been friends for a long time, and she would hate to see a rift between them.

'I asked her round tonight,' said Nicola, 'then I thought we could go down to the youth club.'

'Should you be doing that if you haven't been to school?' queried Kate.

Nicola threw her a withering look. 'You're as bad as Bev—that's what she said. Anyway, she doesn't want to go.'

Kate frowned. There was something in her daughter's tone that suggested all was far from well between the two girls. Then in an attempt to brighten her up she said, 'Never mind, I'll ring Auntie Fran later and we'll arrange something for the weekend.'

Nicola nodded, but Kate was far from happy as she watched her wander upstairs to her bedroom. She had the feeling all was not well with her daughter, but she couldn't put her finger on what was wrong. Maybe it was simply the after-effects from her accident and she would be all right after a weekend enjoying herself with her cousins. She and Nicola had always been close, but just lately Nicola had seemed secretive and less inclined to discuss things with her.

After they had eaten and were watching the news on the television the subject of motor racing came up when the sports announcer mentioned the Le Mans Grand Prix.

'Whatever made you tell Tom Beresford you were interested in motor racing?' asked Kate.

'Because I am,' replied Nicola calmly.

'Well, I haven't been aware of it. Since when have you. . .?'

'I've always thought it was exciting—besides, I wanted to say something intelligent to Tom.'

Kate stared at her daughter. Surely she couldn't be developing a crush on the locum? She was only a child. She stirred restlessly and stood up, then for a moment she looked down at her daughter as she lay sprawled on the sofa. Nicola had grown in the last year and was almost as tall as she, her hair she wore permed into the latest tousled style that was so popular among her friends, and it framed her heart-shaped face. Her grey almond-shaped eyes slanted tantalisingly and her long shapely limbs were lightly tanned. Quite suddenly Kate saw her in a new light.

Uneasily she moved into the kitchen just as the phone started ringing. It was her sister Fran.

'So are you and Nicky coming over?' asked Fran after they'd exchanged hellos.

'When did you have in mind?' asked Kate.

'Well, I thought tomorrow, then stay over until Sunday. You could go back after lunch.'

'That would be fine, Fran,' Kate heard herself say, 'except that I have an awful lot to do tomorrow. I have so much to catch up on, what with being away for a week.'

'That's no problem. Ron's going to the Garden Centre in the morning. He could pick Nicky up and bring her back here, then you could come over and join us for lunch on Sunday. How about that?'

'That would be fine, Fran. Thanks very much. It'll do Nicky good to spend a weekend with your three.'

Moments later when she replaced the receiver Kate found her hand was trembling.

The following morning, after her brother-in-law had picked Nicola up and the house was quiet again, Kate made a determined effort and flung herself into the paperwork and correspondence that had mounted up in her absence, but once again she found it impossible to concentrate. She even welcomed the interruption when Lottie called in to collect her glasses which she'd left on the kitchen shelf the previous day, and she persuaded her to stay and have coffee.

'Is Nicky all right this morning?' asked Lottie as she sipped her coffee.

'Yes, she's fine now. The lump on her head has gone down and her arm is better. She's gone over to my sister's for the weekend.'

'And what about you?' Lottie's usually gruff tone had softened.

'Me?' Kate looked up in surprise afraid for one wild moment that Lottie knew what was going on in her mind. Afraid she knew the real reason she hadn't gone to her sister's. But that was ridiculous, she told herself; how could Lottie know what she had been thinking? And besides, the reason she hadn't gone had been because she had too much work to do. Lottie's next words confirmed this.

'Yes, you work far too hard, Mrs Riley. You should have more time off.'

Kate shrugged. 'That's easier said than done. My

workload at the centre seems to get more and more. . .' She narrowed her eyes. 'Talking of the centre, did you make an appointment, Lottie?'

The older woman sniffed, then shook her head. 'No, I didn't. I'll wait until Dr Scott gets back.'

'But she may not be back for some time.'

'How long?' Lottie frowned.

'It could be a month or even more. Look, why don't you go and see Dr Beresford? He really is very nice.'

'That may well be so, but like I said, I don't want to see no man. It's embarrassing.' Lottie stared down into her cup as she spoke.

'Is it something you could tell me about?' asked Kate gently, then seeing the woman's dubious expression she went on quickly, 'I know I'm not a doctor, but I am a trained nurse.'

That seemed to decide Lottie, for as Kate was only too aware, while she didn't begin to understand what her work as a psychotherapist involved, she did relate to the fact that Kate was also a nurse.

'It's me bowels,' she said at last.

'You mean constipation?' asked Kate.

'Sometimes, but more often than not, it's the other way, if you know what I mean. What's really been worrying me is the bleeding.' She glanced at Kate from beneath her brows as if she feared her reaction, then looked quickly down into her cup again.

'Has there been much bleeding, Lottie?'

Lottie nodded. 'Every time I go to the lavatory.'

Kate stood up and in as matter-a-fact a tone as she could she said, 'You really will have to see a doctor about this, Lottie. It probably isn't anything to worry about, but you should get it checked out, and I don't think it should wait until Dr Scott gets back.'

'But. . .'

'I know it's embarrassing. Would you like me to tell Dr Beresford what you've told me so that at least he'll have some idea what it's all about?'

'Would you do that?' Lottie looked up hopefully.

'Of course I will, and I'll get you an appointment for Monday.'

After Lottie had gone Kate abandoned all further attempts at her paperwork and put one of her favourite opera discs into her CD player, then she began to tend and water her large collection of houseplants.

It was only when she hesitated before going out into the yard to water the flowers in the window-boxes that she realised she was consciously waiting for the phone to ring and was afraid that if she went into the yard she might not be able to hear it.

Tom had said he would ring at lunchtime. She had, of course, already decided not to go to dinner with him, but it was only courteous to take his call and tell him so herself.

She prepared a light lunch, only to find her appetite had completely disappeard, then when the phone did finally ring she almost jumped out of her skin.

As she spoke into the receiver, giving her number, her stomach began to churn, then as she heard Susan Rayner's voice on the other end she felt quite weak with a mixture of relief and anxiety.

Bernard's wife had rung to invite her and Nicola to a party the following weekend. They chatted for a time, but all the while Kate was wondering whether Tom was trying to get through.

When she hung up she stared at the phone, expecting it, almost willing it to ring again, but it remained silent. Why was she reacting like this? Angrily she turned away from the phone — then jumped again as the doorbell rang. Whoever could it be? She would have to get rid of them quickly in case the phone rang again. She ran through into the lounge and tugged open the front door.

Tom Beresford stood on the step.

Kate stared at him blankly, then when he smiled, she said, 'You said you'd phone.' It came out almost accusingly, and she glanced back into the house as she said it, almost as if she still expected the phone to ring.

'Sorry,' he said half jokingly, half apologetic. 'I was in the area and I called on the off-chance.'

'You're on call today?'

'Only until five o'clock. . .you didn't go to your sister's, then?'

'No. . .' She paused, wildly searching for an excuse. 'I had things to do,' she finished lamely.

'And Nicola?' Tom smiled, and his teeth looked very white against his tanned face.

'Nicola?' She frowned. Why did he want to know about Nicola?

'Yes. Has she gone to see her cousins?'

'Oh yes — yes, she has.' Kate took a deep breath and felt her tension begin to ebb a little.

'Aren't you going to ask me in?' he asked.

'What?. . .' She blinked. 'Oh, yes. Of course — I'm sorry, Tom. You caught me unawares.' She stood aside and watched helplessly as Tom strolled into her home.

'Nice little place you have here,' he said, looking round at the comfortable living area and the kitchen beyond. 'Have you been here long?'

'Five years.'

'Just Nicola and you.'

'Just Nicola and me.'

'Isn't that *La Traviata*?' He nodded towards her CD player.

She looked up quickly. 'You like opera?'

He shrugged. 'Not especially. I'm a jazz man myself.'

'Oh.' She was faintly disappointed. Brian hadn't shared her love for opera either.

'I went to some marvellous jazz sessions in Boston,' he went on, stepping towards her small piano as he spoke and lifting up one of the silver-framed photographs from its top. It was one of Nicola taken when she was ten years old. He studied it intently for a moment. 'She must take after her father,' he said, looking up.

His eyes met hers and Kate swallowed. 'Yes, she does.'

He replaced the photograph. 'Do you play?' he asked, indicating the piano.

'Sometimes. Nicola was having lessons.'

'Was?'

'Yes, but she gave up about a year ago.'

'That's a pity.'

She nodded. 'I know, but it wouldn't have done any good to force her to continue. This way at least it was her choice, and there's a good chance she'll come back to it when she's older. . .at the moment she's more interested in pop music.'

'And what about you? Do you like pop music? Or come to that, do you like jazz?'

'I don't mind it. . .'

'That's good.'

'Why?' She looked curiously at him.

'You'll see.' He smiled, then quickly, before she could comment, he said, 'It can't be easy bringing up a teenager on your own and trying to keep up a career.'

'It isn't,' she admitted, wondering if once again she detected a tinge of reproach in his tone as if he considered she shouldn't be attempting both. 'But we get by. Can I get you anything to drink?' she asked, suddenly remembering her manners.

'No. I really can't stop—I'm on my way to a call. One of Ruth Scott's terminal cancer patients.'

Kate was suddenly reminded of Lottie. 'I was talking to another of Ruth's patients earlier,' she said. 'She was all for waiting for Ruth to come back before coming to the centre, but I persuaded her to come and see you.'

'Sounds as if she's reluctant. I hope you told her I won't eat her. Who is she?'

'Her name is Lottie Downer. She comes here to help me with the chores, in fact she's been an absolute treasure over the years, helping out with Nicola and that sort of thing. Actually she's very shy about coming to you, or to any man, with her problem.'

'Do you know what her problem is?' he asked.

'Yes. I also told her I'd put you in the picture before her appointment.'

'So what are her symptoms?'

'Occasional constipation, but mostly, frequent loose motions with blood present in the stools. I thought it sounded like ulcerative colitis. . .'

'That was your diagnosis?' He raised one eyebrow and she noted a gleam of amusement in the grey eyes.

'Of course not.' She flushed. 'I told her you'd need to examine her.'

'And probably send her for further investigation, by the sounds of it.' He paused. 'I was just interested in how a psychotherapist comes up with answers.'

'My answer had nothing to do with psycho-therapy,' said Kate, 'it came more from my nursing experience, especially my three years on a surgi-cal ward.'

He stared at her with apparent renewed interest. 'I didn't know you were a nurse.'

'It sounds as if I've just gone up in your estimation,' she remarked.

'Not at all. I was merely. . .'

'So just what do you have against psychotherapists?' Kate demanded.

'What do you mean?'

'I thought I detected an aversion yesterday.'

'Yesterday?' He frowned. 'Didn't I say I thought psychotherapy had its place?'

'You did, but I thought you were implying that it was a very limited place.'

'You completely misread my meaning.' He glanced at his watch. 'I think we need to explore this fascinating discussion further, but it will have to be later. As I said, I only called in because I happened to be in the area and to tell you that I'll pick you up at seven-thirty.'

'Seven-thirty?'

'Yes, for dinner. Don't tell me you'd forgotten.'

'I didn't think we'd agreed on anything.'

'I understood your only reason for possible refusal was if you were going to be at your sister's,' said Tom. 'As you haven't gone. . .'

'I said I didn't go because I had things to do.'

'I'm sure you'll get everything done before seven-thirty.'

She allowed her eyes to meet his then, and from what she saw there she knew he wasn't going to take no for an answer.

Normally, arrogance in a man annoyed Kate, but as she stood in her doorway and watched Tom drive away, in spite of her earlier decision to keep their relationship purely professional, she found it difficult to suppress her excitement.

CHAPTER FOUR

THE feeling of excitement persisted throughout the afternoon and while she was getting ready to go out, and if she was wary of it, Kate found at the same time that she wasn't too eager to dismiss it. After all, it had been a very long time since any man had made her feel this way. The fact that the man in question just happened to look like her ex-husband she tried to put out of her mind. That it was this that had attracted her to Tom Beresford in the first place, she had no doubt, but she was becoming increasingly aware that he in turn was very attracted to her, and for Kate that was a far stronger aphrodisiac than any nostalgic similarity.

The weather was warm, and she dressed with care, choosing a full skirted, floral-printed dress in a softly silky material. She didn't know where Tom would be taking her, maybe one of the smart new foreign restaurants in West Chillerton, or perhaps he was planning a trip to London, but whichever it was she wanted to be appropriately dressed. Her hair she wore loose, brushing it so that it curved smoothly beneath her jawline; her jewellery was plain, pearl earrings and choker, and her perfume the sophisticated fragrance she always wore.

At last she was satisfied, but when Tom arrived

50

she took one look at the casual way he was dressed and wondered if she'd made a mistake. He didn't appear to be wearing a tie and his dark patterned shirt was open at the neck, but when he turned to look at her as she walked out to the car, she couldn't fail to recognise his admiration as he allowed his gaze to wander over her. And when she took her place beside him, a closer look revealed the knife-edge creases in his beige trousers and the expensive cut of his jacket.

He drove out of West Chillerton and on to the London-bound dual carriageway, but after about ten miles, on the outskirts of Kingston-upon-Thames, he left the main road and headed for the river bank. As they parked the car and strolled along the wide embankment Kate imagined he was taking her to one of the riverside pubs.

Several motorboats and pleasure craft were moored along the embankment, and as they approached a particularly large one Kate caught the strains of music.

'You did say you didn't mind jazz, didn't you?' Tom had stopped and was smiling at her.

The boat was an old paddle steamer, its name, *Medina Queen*, emblazoned on its side. She had quite obviously been lovingly restored, her cream and scarlet paintwork fresh and her brass fittings gleaming in the evening light. The gangway was covered by a striped canvas awning. Tom stood aside, then with a flourish indicated for Kate to board the vessel.

They were greeted by a middle-aged man in uniform who shook Tom's hand, and from their conversation Kate guessed this wasn't Tom's first visit. Lured by the music, she followed Tom below deck to the main saloon, where further investigation revealed a bar, a small dance floor and the jazz band which Kate later learnt was a resident feature of the club. As she waited for Tom to buy drinks she noticed that other members of the staff also greeted him as if they knew him, and fleetingly she wondered who else he had brought there.

They listened to the band for a while, and Kate, even with her inexperience of jazz, recognised it as being very good, then they strolled back on deck and sat down at one of the small tables.

She smiled at Tom over the rim of her glass. 'Something tells me you've been here before,' she said.

'How did you guess? I hope you like it.'

She leaned forward so that she could see down-river; willows edged the banks, dipping their branches into the water, and swans glided between other craft that drifted lazily by. On the embankment couples strolled hand in hand, a church clock somewhere in the town struck the hour, and from below deck there came the haunting strains of a saxophone.

'It's quite beautiful,' she said simply.

'I discovered it by chance one evening,' Tom told her.

She glanced up in surprise. 'You live near here?'

He nodded. 'My home is in Kingston, or I suppose I should say it *was* in Kingston. I gave up the tenancy while I was in the States. I'd been staying with my family in north London, then when I took this locum post Bernard found me a flat in West Chillerton. It's only temporary, of course, until I go back to the States.'

'What research were you involved with in the States?' Suddenly Kate found she wanted to know more about him.

'It was with Mereschell, the pharmaceutical company. It was part of a huge programme concerned with new treatment for all forms of arthritis. As you know, Mereschell already produce several different types of anti-inflammatory drugs, and their scientists are working on something new. It was fascinating work, involving a detailed survey of people from many parts of the world and from every walk of life. We studied a cross-section of these people, everything from hereditary factors and their lifestyle to diet and the drugs they'd taken. Our findings are still being formulated, and a report is due later this year. I think it will make interesting reading, with one or two widely held beliefs exploded — I can't wait to see how it will be received.'

'I thought you said you weren't going back to Boston,' remarked Kate.

'I'm not. A member of the team I was working with at Mereschell has offered me a partnership in the practice I mentioned in Philadelphia.'

A partnership, thought Kate — that meant he

would be going for good. She glanced at him from beneath her lashes and was suddenly struck by how young and enthusiastic he seemed, and for the first time she was really aware of the difference in their ages. His enthusiasm for his new venture reminded her of her own when she had been about to embark on her psychotherapy career. Had that enthusiasm gone? She was startled by the thought. Of course it hadn't. She was as much committed to her career as she had always been—it was just that lately it had seemed to be all work and with no time for anything else in her life.

At that moment a waiter appeared on deck, and Tom leaned forward. 'I thought it might be nice to eat out here as it's so warm, is that all right with you?' he asked.

'Yes, it would be a shame to waste this glorious weather,' Kate agreed.

They ordered seafood; fresh lobster, crab and king prawns, then, while they were waiting for their meal to arrive, Kate said, 'I must admit it's nice to get away from West Chillerton and the surgery, and to relax for a while.'

'Do I take it from that you don't get out very often?' queried Tom

'My social life has been pretty non-existent just lately. I manage an occasional trip to the opera, but any other treats tend to be for Nicola. My work seems to take up the rest of my time.'

'Ah, yes, your work. We were discussing the merits of psychotherapy earlier, weren't we?'

'Yes, and I thought you'd implied that it had a very limited place in healing,' she said.

'And I said you'd misread my meaning.' He raised one eyebrow quizzically, then paused as the waiter arrived with their meal.

When they were alone again Kate stared steadily at him across the table. 'So what was your meaning?' she asked.

'I can see I shall have to tread carefully here,' he said as he helped himself to salad. 'I think that both counselling and psychotherapy can play an important part in the healing process, but I can also feel there's a danger that they can get out of control.'

'What do you mean?' Kate set down her knife and fork and stared at him.

'I think that medical conditions are sometimes in danger of being missed because they're being attributed to psychological problems.'

'And I think there are many medical conditions that have been wrongly diagnosed and treated when psychotherapy would have revealed the true nature of the problem.'

'You could be right—in some cases. But don't forget, I've just been working in a country where folk consult their analyst before deciding what colour curtains to buy.'

Kate laughed in spite of her earlier indignation, and Tom joined in her laughter.

'I wouldn't like to see things reach those proportions in this country,' he said, taking a mouthful of wine.

'You sound concerned about the future of this country, and yet you're leaving. Why?' she asked curiously.

He shrugged. 'An opportunity presented itself. It'll be a challenge.' He paused. 'A change is as good as a rest. Talking of changes, how did you come to give up nursing and get into psychotherapy?'

'My interest in psychotherapy came about from personal experience,' she said quietly. Tom remained silent, but his interest was apparent from his expression, and for the first time ever Kate found herself talking about her own counselling. 'It was after my divorce,' she went on slowly. 'For a long time I seemed to be floundering around trying to make sense of what had happened to me. I couldn't come to terms with it. I felt a failure, that it was all my fault and that because of my inadequacy I'd deprived Nicola of her father.'

'How long were you married?' he asked.

'Just over three years, but we were only together for about eighteen months. It was a disaster almost from the start, and after Nicola was born things went from bad to worse.'

'Do you know what the problem was?'

'I do now, but I didn't at the time. We didn't take long enough getting to know each other. What I didn't realise was that Brian had an ego problem. One woman wasn't enough for him. I wasn't mature enough to handle that. . .' Kate shrugged. 'After the divorce, a colleague saw what I was going through and suggested counselling. I refused at first, I suppose I couldn't think of myself as being the type of person who needed counselling—most people think that, you know——' she gave a tight little smile '— but it was only after I'd had several sessions of counselling that I began to see things in their true perspective and stopped taking the entire blame for what had happened.'

'And you think it was this that triggered your own interest in that field?'

'I know it was,' she replied simply. 'And I've since realised that the best therapists have themselves undergone personal therapy or analysis.'

'Have you seen your husband since the divorce?'

Kate shook her head and wondered what Tom would say if he knew just how many memories of Brian he had stirred in the last couple of days. 'No, he emigrated to New Zealand shortly afterwards.'

'Doesn't he keep in touch with Nicola?'

'No,' she said bitterly. 'He was never interested in his daughter. I did hear that he is married again and has another family.'

'And what about Nicola? Does it bother her that her father doesn't want to know?'

Kate hesitated, then slowly she said, 'I sometimes think I've convinced myself that it doesn't bother her, then quite unexpectedly she'll mention him. Like she did to you,' her gaze flickered to him, 'and at the time you were almost a stranger to her. I may have to watch that she's not going to suffer a severe rejection reaction as she gets older.'

'I wouldn't read anything too sinister into the fact

that she mentioned it to me, if I were you,' he advised.

'But it does happen. One of my clients was forty-two before she realised. . . Why are you smiling?'

'Because I asked her about her father.'

'But why should you have done that?' queried Kate.

'It was after her accident, if you remember. She'd already said you were away, and I simply asked her where her father was. It was a natural enough question in the circumstances, although I must admit I was a bit taken aback when she said he was in New Zealand, but you can't read any more than that into it, Kate.'

'So now you're saying my psychotherapy training has gone into overdrive and I'm reading something that isn't there into the situation?'

'I'm not saying that at all. . .'

'Either that or I shouldn't have gone off on that seminar and left Nicola.'

He stared at her, then sighed. 'Kate, you're being far too sensitive—I hadn't thought anything of the kind. In fact, I admire the way you seemed to have brought Nicola up single-handed and got on so well in your career at the same time.'

Kate took a deep breath, then slowly let it go. 'I'm sorry, Tom,' she said at last. 'You're quite right, I am very sensitive, especially where Nicola's concerned, and I frequently find it difficult striking the right balance between my work and spending time with her.'

'And in the midst of all this you've forgotten how to be yourself.'

'What do you mean?' She looked startled for a moment, and he remained silent as a group of young people appeared on deck and sat down at another of the tables. Then unexpectedly he stood up and, looking down at her, he held out his hand.

'Come on, let's walk for a while.'

He took her hand and drew her to her feet. Kate waited while he paid the bill, then they left the boat and strolled along the embankment. The light was beginning to fade, the shadows deepening beneath the overhanging willows where the water looked dark and mysterious with barely a ripple to disturb its surface.

Tom took her hand again and they strolled in silence for a while.

'What did you mean?' asked Kate at last. 'About forgetting to be myself?'

He didn't answer immediately, instead appearing to be intently watching a family of moorhens drifting towards the far bank of the river, then, just when she was beginning to think he hadn't heard, he turned towards her. 'I get the impression that you're so busy trying to be the perfect mother and the successful psychotherapist that Kate, the woman, has somehow become trapped inside you.'

'But being those things are me...they're the factors of my life that make up what I am. What more could I want?'

They had stopped, and Kate was looking up at him, frowning slightly as she waited for his reply.

'How about this?' he said softly, and reaching out his hand he gently touched the side of her face, tilting it slightly, then, before she had time to think about what was happening, he leaned forward and kissed her.

It took her by surprise, and she stepped back hurriedly and stared at him in amazement.

'Hasn't there been any room for that in your life?' he asked quietly.

Slowly she shook her head. 'No, there hasn't. I put that out of my mind a very long time ago,' she said shakily. The touch of his lips, brief as it had been, had stirred something in her memory, something pleasurable that had been shut away for far too long.

'Maybe that's what's missing,' he said, maybe you should bring it back into your life.'

'I'm not sure I want that again in my life,' she said slowly.

They walked on, and when they came to the towpath at the end of the embankment they were forced to walk in single file to allow another couple to pass them. Tom stopped and looked back, forcing Kate to do the same. The boy and girl had walked on, their arms around each other.

'Everyone needs somebody to love,' he said simply.

'And what about you?' she retorted.

'What about me?'

They walked on, and he slid his arm around her shoulders. Kate let it stay, liking the feel of it. 'Well, you seemed to have done a good job analysing me and what's missing in my life, now it's my turn. Do you have somebody to love, Tom Beresford?'

She glanced at him when he remained silent, and the expression she caught on his face almost made her wish she hadn't asked. He too had suffered, and she recognised that look of pain in his eyes — hadn't she seen it often enough in the course of her work? She wondered whether he would try to deny it.

'It wouldn't be any good trying to hide anything from you, you're far too perceptive. Yes, I had someone to love,' he said honestly. 'She was a doctor at the hospital where I did my training. We lived together for a couple of years.'

'So what went wrong?'

'Her career was more important to her. She wanted to go for her consultancy, and she didn't want to make any personal commitment.'

'You were hurt.' It was a statement, and he nodded.

'Yes, I was hurt.'

'So what did you do?'

'I went to the States.' He glanced sharply at Kate. 'You're going to say I ran away from the situation.'

'I wasn't going to say anything of the kind. It isn't for me to make judgements.'

'Maybe not. But I know it's what you're thinking.'

'Do you think you ran away?' she asked curiously.

He shrugged. 'Probably. But at least I haven't

shut myself off from the possibility of other relationships.'

'I bet you haven't.' She was laughing now, and he tightened his grip on her shoulders so that it was almost a hug.

Suddenly she realised she felt totally at ease with him.

They walked for a long time in the gathering dusk, talking of their lives, their families and their jobs, then when they reached a stile where the towpath opened out on to water meadows Tom suggested they turned back.

By the time they reached the embankment it was almost dark, and the reflected lights from the *Medina Queen* shimmered on the water. People lined the decks now and the music from below filled the air.

Kate glanced at Tom and saw the animation on his face as they drew closer. 'Are we going back on board?' she asked, instinct telling her it was what he wanted.

'Would you like to?' He sounded surprised but pleased.

'Why not?' she smiled.

'All right. One last drink.'

She followed him aboard, and this time they went below deck to the bar in the saloon where the jazz band was playing. It was very crowded, although no one appeared to be dancing, instead they stood watching the musicians. Kate and Tom joined them after he had bought them both a shandy.

Like the rest of the boat the saloon bar had been cleverly restored to give an impression of how it had been in days gone by. The varnished wood-panelled walls were hung with prints of antique maps and steam-powered vessels, while the benches beneath the portholes had been upholstered in deep ruby velvet. The atmosphere was dense and smoky, the lights dim, and as the saxophonist went into a solo routine a ripple of excitement spread through the crowd.

They set their glasses down on a table, then Tom stood behind Kate and putting his arms around her held her against him.

'Listen to him,' he murmured. 'It's Count "Mallow" Warwick — he's brilliant — just listen to the way he plays that sax!'

Kate leaned against him, amused by his enthusiasm, but as she listened she found her own senses stimulated by the music, then gradually she became aware of another sensation — of how content she was to be with Tom, to feel his arms around her and to know once again the pressure of a male body against hers.

They stayed for another hour, and when finally they left the boat and strolled hand in hand to the car the music reverberated in Kate's head.

'I can't remember when I enjoyed myself so much,' she said as she took her place beside him in the car.

'I'm relieved to hear you say so. I had my doubts about my choice when you said you were into opera.'

He threw her a quick glance. 'Then when I saw how exquisite you looked I thought you might be expecting some chic restaurant and that the atmosphere on the boat wouldn't be sophisticated enough for you.'

Kate smiled, pleased that he had liked the way she looked. They drove in silence then, and she wriggled into the corner of her seat so that she could watch Tom; the strong lines of his profile just visible in the light from the dashboard, the lowered brows as he concentrated on the road ahead, the straight nose and slightly flaring nostrils, the finely shaped mouth with its full lower lip and the firm line of his jaw. He did resemble Brian, there was no denying that, but during the time they had spent together she had come to realise that that was all it was—a physical resemblance. In other ways Tom was nothing like Brian.

When they reached the mews Tom drew the car into the yard and without switching off the engine turned and looked at her.

'Aren't you coming in?' she asked softly.

He switched off the engine.

CHAPTER FIVE

KATE lay watching the patterns on the ceiling formed by the early morning sunlight. The bedroom window was open, and in the distance the sound of church bells reminded her that it was Sunday. Later she would drive to her sister's to join Nicola. Fran would cook a huge Sunday roast, then afterwards they would take the dogs for a long walk on the heath before she and Nicola set out for home. She hoped Nicola was having a good time with her cousins — two boys older than her and a girl a little younger — maybe she would want to tell her all about what they had been doing, just as she used to do when she was small.

Kate sighed and carefully turned her head so as not to disturb the sleeping man beside her.

He was lying on his side facing her, one arm flung protectively across her, the thin cotton sheet barely covering his naked body. His thick, wheat-coloured hair was tousled, making him appear vulnerable and even younger than he was.

She sighed, wishing for a moment that she was ten years younger, although the difference in their ages certainly hadn't seemed to worry Tom. If she was truthful she was slightly shocked at what had happened. If anyone had told her a couple of days before that she would be sleeping with a man she'd only just met, she would have dismissed the idea as ludicrous.

But Tom Beresford wasn't just any man. He was different. And she'd known it from the moment she'd set eyes on him.

Their lovemaking had been spontaneous, the inevitable conclusion of the evening they had spent together. He had been both tender and passionate, arousing in Kate long-forgotten desires, and in the end taking her to heights she had never before reached—not even in the early days with Brian. With him, Kate had done all the giving, but Tom's main objective seemed to have been to give her as much pleasure as possible, with his own needs taking second place.

She had thought no further than the moment, but now, in the light of morning, her mind raced ahead. What would happen now? Tom was a colleague, and it was a well-known fact that Bernard frowned upon relationships within the practice, and then there was Nicola; what would her reaction be to her mother sleeping with Tom Beresford? Kate shuddered slightly at the thought and turned her mind to more practical matters as she tried to remember what she had in the house to eat.

'What are you thinking about?'

She jumped and looked quickly at Tom, to find that he was awake and was watching her.

'I was wondering what I was going to give you for breakfast.'

'What do you have?' he asked.

'Not very much, I'm afraid. We're not great breakfast eaters in this house, we belong to the toast and cereal brigade.'

'I fancy a forbidden breakfast.' He stretched luxuriously, then said, 'Tell you what, you get the coffee on and I'll nip down to the corner shop and get some bacon and eggs, and mushrooms, if they have them.'

'All right.' Kate turned and would have slipped out of bed, but Tom tightened the sheets around her. She looked back at him.

'Not yet, though,' he said softly.

'But I thought you said. . .'

'First things first.' He pulled her towards him. 'There are some things that just can't wait — this being one of them.' He eased his body over hers, catching her wrists and imprisoning them on the pillow on either side of her head.

She only had time for a little gasp of delight before his mouth closed over hers and she gave herself up to the urgent demands of his body.

Later, while Tom cooked bacon and mushrooms, Kate poured fresh orange juice and made toast and coffee. She watched him, still faintly disbelieving as he stood before her cooker breaking eggs into the frying pan. He had turned back the cuffs of his shirt and his hair was still damp from the shower, and when he turned, the dark stubble on his jaw gave him a slightly rakish appearance.

They enjoyed a leisurely breakfast, for all the

world like any married couple, and it wasn't until they cleared away and tidied the kitchen and the bedroom that questions began to hang unspoken in the air.

It was Tom who finally broke the silence that had grown between them and was threatening to take over and destroy what they had discovered.

'So where do we go from here?' he asked quietly, leaning back against the sink and folding his arms.

Kate shook her head. 'I've no idea. I can hardly believe it's happened.'

'Do you want it to continue?'

'I'm not sure. It will pose problems at work. . . and then there's Nicola. . .'

'That isn't what I asked. I asked what you wanted.'

She shook her head. 'I honestly don't know, Tom. I never imagined I was the type of person to indulge in a one-night stand, but on the other hand, I'm pretty certain I don't want any permanent commitment.'

'Hey, why so serious?' He leaned forward and looked into her face. 'I wasn't talking about permanent commitment either.'

'Of course. . .you're going away, I'd forgotten.' The thought hit her like a blow in the stomach. 'What, then. . .?'

'Why not just enjoy each other's company for as long as it lasts?'

'You mean a sort of "no strings" affair?'

'Why not?' When she still hesitated, he went on,

'It seems the sensible option. Listen, Kate, what's happened between us—I think it was special, meant to be, if you like, but I understand that you don't want to launch into a deep relationship any more than I do. Don't you think it was special?'

She sighed. 'Yes, Tom, I do. It was very special, completely unexpected.'

'So why not keep it that way for a while, at least until I go back to the States? And if you think it'll cause problems, then we keep it quiet.'

'You think we'll be able to?' She looked dubious.

'We can try.'

He had left soon after that, and it was with a feeling of unreality that Kate drove to her sister's, but for the rest of the day all she could do was wish the time away until the next morning when she could go to work and see Tom again. She felt so different that she was sure that if not Fran, then Nicola would notice, but neither of them seemed aware of any change in her.

Nicola appeared happier and had spent most of the weekend with her cousins on their boat on the river, and when later they drove back to West Chillerton she chattered to Kate about all they had done.

Somehow Kate got through the rest of the day, but she found it incredibly difficult not to mention Tom to Nicola, and she found herself wanting to tell her daughter all about her trip to the *Medina Queen*. She and Tom had agreed not to mention their relationship to anyone unless they were forced to do so, but deep down Kate knew that wasn't the only reason she wasn't telling her daughter.

On Monday morning Nicola went off to school, and Kate left a note telling Lottie to come into the surgery later in the morning.

When she arrived at the centre Kate was keyed up at the thought of seeing Tom, but she heard one of the receptionists say that Dr Beresford was out on an emergency call, so she had to start her morning's work without seeing him.

Her first client was Robert, a young man who was experiencing problems with claustrophobia and who had been referred to Kate by Bernard. His phobia was beginning to seriously disrupt his life, as his job involved a certain amount of travelling and he was finding it increasingly difficult to use many forms of transport. It was his third visit to Kate, and she was gradually allowing him to talk his way back to his very early childhood to try to identify the reason for his phobia. She then intended using behaviour therapy, during which, after he had reached a deep level of relaxation, she would introduce him to the various situations that terrified him.

At the start of his therapy sessions Robert had seemed suspicious and sceptical, but as he stood up to leave that morning, Kate thought she detected the first indications that she was gaining his trust. He seemed hopeful and optimistic, and didn't flinch when Kate talked of the goal they had set at the start of the sessions—a trip to France with his girlfriend.

Her second client of the morning was Joe, and the moment he walked into the room Kate sensed a change in him. His movements were jerky and his speech erratic.

'Come and sit down, Joe,' she said after he had spent the first five minutes prowling around the room. Then when he was sitting, in an attempt to bring the conversation back to where they had left off at his previous session, she said, 'Would you like to tell me more about the time you started school?'

It seemed, however, that Joe had other ideas about what he wanted to talk about that morning and began a tirade about his stepfather. By the time his session was over Kate felt that instead of making progress he had taken a step backwards. Thoughtfully she watched him leave the room, then her intercom sounded.

'Hello, Lynn?' she answered.

'Kate, there's a lady called Lottie down here. She's asking for you, and she won't tell me what she wants.'

'It's all right, Lynn, I know what it's about. I'll be right down.'

After checking that Tom didn't have a patient with him Kate went into the waiting-room, where she found Lottie sitting nervously on the edge of a chair. 'Hello, Lottie,' she said gently. 'I've arranged for you to see Dr Beresford.'

Lottie looked up quickly, her brown eyes darting from Kate to the consulting-rooms in the corridor.

'Would you like to go in now?' asked Kate.

'Will you come with me, Mrs Riley?'

'If you want me to, certainly I will.'

As Kate lifted her hand to tap on Tom's door she wondered who was the more nervous, Lottie or herself. She hadn't seen him since he'd left her home the previous morning, and she was beginning to wonder if it had all been a dream.

But when she heard his voice telling them to enter, and when she stepped into his room and his grey eyes met hers, she knew that what had happened between them, far from being a dream, had been very real indeed.

Desperately she tried to pull herself together, but her heart seemed to be doing crazy things. 'Dr Beresford,' she heard herself say, 'this is Lottie Downer.'

'Hello, Lottie.' Tom stood up to greet her. 'Come on in, and make yourself comfortable.'

'Lottie has asked me to stay—is that all right, Doctor?' asked Kate.

'Of course it is.' He turned to Lottie. 'I believe you and Mrs Riley are old friends,' he said. 'She's been telling me how much you help her, especially with Nicola.'

It was the best thing he could have said, and Kate was relieved to see that Lottie looked pleased and immediately started to relax.

'Now, Lottie,' Tom went on in a chatty sort of

way, 'Mrs Riley has also been telling me about a few problems you've been having—such as going to the toilet rather more frequently than usual. Would you like to tell me a little more about that? Do you have any pain?'

Kate sat back and let Tom carry on, and by the time he had asked Lottie to undress and lie on the couch in his examination room she was pleased to see that Lottie was chatting to him as if she'd known him for years.

And that's how I feel, thought Kate as she waited while he carried out his examination—as if I've known him for years. She glanced round his room, at his case open on the bench, his pen lying on his desk and his jacket draped casually on the back of his chair, and these personal objects seemed as familiar to her as if she'd been seeing them every day for a lifetime

After Tom had concluded his examination and Lottie had dressed she came back into the consulting room and joined Kate, and they waited while Tom finished writing in Lottie's records.

'Is it anything serious, Doctor?' asked Lottie anxiously as Tom looked up.

'I don't think so, Lottie,' he replied. 'I certainly can't find anything that shouldn't be there. However, the symptoms you're having are distressing, and something must be causing them, even if it's only the fact that you're eating the wrong things. I want you to have some X-rays, Lottie—what we call a barium enema,' he added as he began filling in an X-ray request form.

'What's that?' Lottie looked worried and glanced at Kate.

'It's a substance that they put into your bowel so that when an X-ray is taken the outline of the bowel shows up clearly. But in the meantime, I want you to take one of these diet sheets home with you and keep to it as much as you can. You'll see the diet includes lots of fibre — bran, fruit, wholemeal bread. I'll also give you something to help to ease your symptoms.' He typed a prescription on to the keyboard of his computer. 'You should hear from the hospital fairly quickly, and I want you to come back and see me about a week after your X-ray.' As he finished speaking the computer printed out the prescription, he tore it off and handed it to Lottie.

'Thank you, Doctor.' Lottie stood up, and as Kate followed her from the room she glanced back and gave Tom a brief smile.

She walked to the front door with Lottie. 'That wasn't so bad, was it?' she said.

'Young Nicola was quite right, he isn't like a doctor,' muttered Lottie, and without further explanation she trundled off down the road, leaving Kate smiling and shaking her head.

Moments later she joined the doctors in the staff-room. 'Ah, Kate,' said Bernard, 'I was just inviting Tom to our little party — I believe Susan rang you about it, didn't she?'

'She did indeed,' said Kate. 'I'm looking forward

to it.' She glanced at Tom and seeing the glint of amusement in his eyes she thought how much more she was looking forward to it now that she knew he was going to be there.

'Susan also rang your sister Fran,' Bernard went on. 'She and her husband are coming as well.' He turned to Tom. 'Susan and Kate's sister are old friends,' he explained, 'they went to school together.'

Kate poured herself a coffee, then turned to Tom. 'Thank you for seeing Lottie,' she said quietly.

'My pleasure. She's a nice lady, if a very anxious one.'

'You don't think it's anything sinister?'

'As I said, I couldn't find anything. Your diagnosis of ulcerative colitis could well be correct.' He glanced up as Malcolm came into the room and embarked on a heated discussion with Bernard over the surgery rota. 'On the other hand, maybe her symptoms will turn out to be stress-related or psychological, in which case, I'll refer her to you.'

'I'll believe that the day it happens,' said Kate lightly.

'What?' He raised his eyebrows.

'You referring a patient to me for psychotherapy because you can't find an answer to her problems.'

'Would you do the same for me?'

'Of course,' said Kate quickly. 'In fact, I was about to mention a patient to you. He's registered with Ruth, and he's had psychiatric treatment in the past. He's been coming to me for therapy for some weeks now, and I thought we were making progress, but today I thought he seemed disturbed and may be in need of medication again.'

'When are you seeing him next?' asked Tom.

'Tomorrow.'

'See how he is. If you're concerned, certainly I'll see him—speaking of which,' he went on, then without lowering his voice, said, 'when am I going to see you again?'

Kate's eyes widened and she glanced towards Bernard and Malcolm, but they didn't seem to have noticed anything and were still deeply engrossed in their own conversation. Returning her gaze to Tom, she saw the glint of amusement was back in his eyes.

'Leave it to me,' she murmured. 'I'll see what I can arrange.'

That evening when Kate got home she was pleased to find Beverley and Nicola doing their homework together. Maybe she'd only imagined the rift she'd thought there had been between the two girls. When she was preparing their evening meal Beverley went home, and Nicola wandered into the kitchen.

'How was Tom today?' she asked as she helped herself to a handful of cheese that Kate was grating for an omelette.

Kate paused. 'He was OK—I think. I didn't see much of him, actually, but he seems to be settling in all right. Susan Rayner's invited him to her party. . .' She hesitated as an idea struck her. 'As a matter of fact, I thought I'd ask him here for a meal, maybe one night this week.'

'That's not fair!' Nicola had stopped eating the cheese and was staring at Kate.

'What isn't?' Kate blinked.

'Tom's my friend, not yours.'

Kate's hesitation was barely perceptible. 'In that case, you invite him,' she said firmly. Nicola stared at her. 'Go on, go and phone him now.' Kate glanced at the kitchen clock. 'He'll still be at the centre.'

'Can Beverley come as well?' Nicola slid off the kitchen stool.

'If she wants to.'

'All right, then.' Nicola disappeared into the hall, but she didn't close the door, and Kate heard her dial a number. There was a silence, then she heard her say, 'Tom? It's Nicola Riley here.' Another silence, then, 'Yes, I'm fine now, thank you. I'm phoning to ask if you'd like to come to supper one night this week.' There was a further pause, then Kate heard her daughter say, 'Well, how about tomorrow night? Yes, that'll be fine. See you about seven, then? Bye.'

She was smiling triumphantly when she strolled back into the kitchen.

'What did he say?' asked Kate.

'He said he'd be delighted. What will we have to eat?'

'That's your problem, he's your guest,' said Kate smoothly.

'Oh, Mum!'

Kate grinned. 'I expect we'll think of something,' she said, then added sharply, 'Nicola, will you please stop eating that cheese, there won't be any left for the omelette.'

'Sorry—I'm hungry.'

'Didn't you have a snack when you came home from school?'

'I couldn't see anything I fancied. There was only some bacon in the fridge. What did you buy that for?'

Kate stopped, the grater poised in one hand, a lump of cheese in the other, and stared at her daughter. 'Bacon?' she said weakly, and when her daughter nodded, she mumbled, 'Oh, I fancied a bacon sandwich, that's all.'

'You? A bacon sandwich? And you always going on about cholesterol? Tut, tut, Mother!' Nicola laughed. 'I think I'll phone Beverley now—I'm sure she'll want to come. I've been telling her all about how dishy Tom is.'

'I hope the pair of you won't embarrass the poor man,' said Kate.

'As if we would!' Nicola sniffed in disgust, and went back to the phone.

'I've had a charming invitation to supper,' said Tom, putting his head round Kate's door the following morning.

'Is that a fact?' Her eyes widened innocently, then they both laughed.

'So what happened?' He came right into the room then and perched on the edge of her desk. Her heart seemed to beat a little faster.

'I simply mentioned quite casually to Nicola that I thought I'd invite you to supper, and she practically flew at me, saying that you were her friend and not mine — almost a case of she saw you first.'

'I wondered if it was something like that when I answered the phone, so I played along, didn't even mention you,' said Tom.

'I thought she had us sussed afterwards,' said Kate, pulling a face.

'Why?' Tom looked up quietly, half amused.

'She found the remains of the bacon in the fridge.'

'So? I don't understand.'

'I never buy bacon.'

He stared at her, then chuckled. 'Oh dear, "what a tangled web we weave". . .'

'"When first we practise to deceive",' she finished the quotation. 'I know, but seriously, Tom, we'll have to tread carefully where Nicola is concerned.'

'Why?'

'I'm pretty certain she has a crush on you.'

'What!' He looked astounded.

'Yes. Is it so improbable?'

'Well, I'm flattered, of course, but. . .' he shrugged helplessly '. . .she's only a. . .' He trailed off.

'Only a child?' asked Kate, raising her eyebrows. 'I think I've been deluding myself on that score as well, but Nicola in fact is at a very vulnerable age, at a time where she's still involved with things of her childhood but where her body is telling her she's almost a woman. I've been trying to see things from her point of view, Tom. A handsome young doctor rescues her after an accident, pays her lots of attention and tells her all about his exciting life in the States and his glamorous pastime, which just happens to be motor racing—honestly, Tom, you can't blame her. It would turn the head of any young girl!'

He was laughing as Kate finished, and he looked so handsome that her breath caught in her throat. 'Seriously,' she went on, 'if she found out about us, I don't think she'd ever speak to me again.'

He grew serious again. 'Don't worry, Kate,' he said softly, and reaching out his hand he covered hers, squeezing them. 'Now you've told me, I'll tread very carefully where Nicola's concerned.' He stood up then, and Kate watched him walk to the door, where he paused and looked back. 'Just tell me one thing—I need to know.' He stared intently at her.

'Yes?'

'Did you really mean what you said?'

She frowned. 'I don't understand.'

'About me being young and handsome. . .?' he grinned.

Kate searched around in exasperation, found a folder of papers, but by the time she'd thrown them Tom had ducked out of the room and they hit the closed door.

She laughed, then grew serious, staring at the door. Never mind her daughter, what had Tom

Beresford done to her? She couldn't remember when she'd last felt this way. He'd brought youth, fun and laughter into her life again. Was that so wrong? Surely there could be no harm in it, provided, of course, no one got hurt.

Her intercom suddenly buzzed, and Kate jumped. She pressed the switch and Julie's voice said, 'Kate, did you know your first client has been waiting for fifteen minutes?'

She glanced guiltily at the clock. 'Oh, send her up, please, will you, Julie?' she said.

CHAPTER SIX

JOE didn't turn up for his therapy session that day, and Kate mentioned the fact to Tom at lunchtime.

'I'm a bit concerned about him,' she said.

'Where's he living?'

'In a bedsit in Cromwell Road.'

'Do you want me to pay him a visit?'

'I think someone should check on him,' said Kate. 'Something had obviously upset him yesterday.'

'Perhaps you'd better come with me, Kate,' Tom suggested. 'After all, he knows you and I'm a stranger to him. I've got another call to make in that road, so we'll combine the two.'

The houses in Cromwell Road were old and large. Most had been converted from what had once been the comfortable homes of the affluent into flats and bed-sits which had become run-down and dilapidated.

They eventually found the address listed on the front of Joe's medical records, but when they reached the first floor and rang the doorbell of Flat Five there was no reply. As they turned to leave, however, a woman stuck her head out of another of the doors.

'Watcha want?' she demanded, then before they could answer she went on, 'He ain't in — gone to sign on.'

'Is he all right?' asked Kate.

The woman stared at her. 'He's daft,' she said, tapping her forehead.

'But has he seemed any different to you in the last few days?' asked Tom.

She shrugged. 'No dafter than usual, if that's what you mean.' She turned and went back into her flat, closing the door behind her.

'There isn't any more we can do,' shrugged Tom.

'It just isn't like Joe not to come for his session,' said Kate 'and we don't know for sure he's gone to sign on, do we?' She turned and looked at his closed door again.

'I don't think he's in there,' said Tom, reading her mind. 'That woman must have seen him go out. When's his next session due?'

'Tomorrow,' said Kate.

'See if he turns up for that. If he doesn't, we'll take further steps. But right now, I have a new baby to see.'

Kate waited in the car while Tom made his call on the young mother and her first baby, who had just returned home from hospital. In spite of Tom's reassuring manner she was still uneasy about Joe, but, as he had pointed out, at this stage there was little they could do. Kate found herself hoping that it wouldn't reach a stage where anything would have to be done, but she wished she knew what it was that had triggered the behaviour change in Joe.

She was so locked in her thoughts that she almost missed the girl who walked past the car, then turned in to another of the houses. She was dressed in an ankle-length black skirt and a short beaded jacket. Her red hair flowed from beneath a black felt hat, its brim pulled forward over her nose. It was only as she walked up the path and Kate saw her in profile that she realised with a little jolt that it was Kim — the girl they had seen in the precinct restaurant, the girl who Nicola had said was her friend. Kate wondered idly why she wasn't at school, then Tom came out of the house, ran down the steps, and she forgot the girl as she watched him, marvelling anew at what had happened between them.

'Everything all right?' She turned towards him as he got into the car.

He nodded. 'Yes — beautiful baby, but the mother's having difficulty with feeding. I'll make sure the health visitor goes in later today.' He sat for a moment staring up at the house; the paint on the door and the window frames was peeling and two of the downstairs windows were boarded up. 'The housing situation is desperate,' he commented. 'Thank God it's summer — they only had a one-bar electric fire in there as far as I could see.'

'All these places seem to be the same,' said Kate. 'I just saw Kim go into one.'

'Kim?' he frowned.

'Yes — the girl who came and spoke to Nicola when we were having lunch in the precinct.'

'Oh, yes I remember. Is she a friend? I thought she looked older than Nicola.'

'Apparently they're in the same year at school,' Kate told him.

Tom started the engine and they pulled away. 'Talking of Nicola,' he said, 'am I to pretend this is my first visit to the house tonight?'

Kate hesitated, then said, 'Yes, Tom, I think you must. I don't like deceiving her, but in the circumstances I think it would be for the best.'

'OK, I'll have to make sure I have my wits about me. I have the feeling your daughter's very sharp.'

'Don't I know it!' groaned Kate.

'What I really want to know is, when are we going to spend some time alone?' he asked, taking his eyes from the road for a moment.

His smile made her heart turn over. 'I'm not sure,' she said. 'It's difficult with Nicola being there.'

'Maybe you could come to my flat some time?'

'Yes, maybe,' she replied, knowing this was what she wanted as much as he apparently did.

The opportunity to find out the reason for Joe's change in behaviour came sooner than Kate had anticipated when later that afternoon she encountered his mother coming out of the blood-pressure clinic run by the practice nurse.

When she caught sight of Kate she stopped, seemed about to say something, then put her head down and would have hurried on if Kate hadn't intervened.

'It's Mrs Platt, isn't it?' queried Kate.

The woman looked up, feigning surprise. 'Oh, hello, Mrs Riley,' she said.

'Have you seen Joe today, Mrs Platt?'

'No, not today.' The woman hesitated and glanced round almost furtively as if she expected her son to suddenly materialise.

'Do you think you could spare me a few minutes?' asked Kate, trying to edge the woman towards the stairs.

'Well, I'm in a hurry really. . .'

'It won't take long,' said Kate pleasantly.

Moments later as she closed the door of her consulting-room and bade Mrs Platt take a seat she said, 'I'm a bit concerned about Joe—you see, he didn't keep his appointment today, and that isn't like him.'

The woman shrugged as if that was hardly anything to worry about, but Kate sensed that she was nervous. As if to confirm that fact she began twisting the wedding-ring on her finger.

'When did you last see Joe?' asked Kate, keeping her tone as casual as possible.

'Day before yesterday,' she answered quickly—too quickly.

'And where did you see him? Did you go to his bedsit?'

'No, he. . .he came to the house.'

Kate stared at her in surprise. From her sessions with Joe she knew his stepfather had forbidden him access to the house since he'd been thrown out. 'Did something happen, Mrs Platt, when Joe came to the house? Did something upset him?'

The woman didn't answer, just sat staring down at her thin hands.

'Mrs Platt,' prompted Kate after a while, 'why did Joe go to your house?'

'You can't blame Reg, he warned him not to come . . .and I — well, I've got the other children to think about. . .' Mrs Platt looked up, clearly agitated.

'Reg is your husband, isn't he?' The woman nodded, and Kate went on, 'Did he go for Joe again?'

'Yes,' she answered quickly, then sighed. 'But Joe hit him back this time. . .he's never done that before. Reg has always been jealous of Joe, you see. . .'

'Yes, I know,' said Kate.

Mrs Platt looked up quickly, then shrugged in a helpless way as if suddenly realising that Kate would know everything about her family; how she'd had Joe before she was married, how she'd married Reg Platt when Joe was eight years old and had gone on to have three more children, how Joe and Reg had never got on, how Joe had needed treatment as he got older, first for minor incidents like bed-wetting but later for more serious behaviour problems.

'Why did Joe go back?' asked Kate again.

Mrs Platt sighed. 'He came to see me.'

'Did you find out why? What did he want?'

'He didn't want nothing.' She swallowed. 'He wanted to give me something. . .it was my birthday.'

Kate stared at her. 'You mean Joe came to the house because he had a present for you?'

'Yes.' Mrs Platt nodded but seemed unable to look Kate in the eye.

'What was the present?'

'I think. . . I think it was a cushion. I saw Joe one day in the precinct, I was looking in a shop window, and he came and spoke to me. I was admiring some patchwork cushions. . .like those,' Mrs Platt pointed to the cushion on Kate's chair. 'I think that was what he'd bought.'

'You mean you don't know? He didn't actually give you the present?'

The woman shook her head. 'I saw it, it was the shape of a cushion, it was still wrapped in the bag with the name of the shop on it. . .but Reg. . . Reg wouldn't let him give it to me.'

Kate took a deep breath and somehow refrained from commenting. What Mrs Platt had just described would be enough to upset most people, let alone someone with Joe's history. 'What happened then?' she asked quietly, already knowing the answer.

'Reg went for Joe when he refused to go, but like I said, this time Joe hit Reg back — they had quite a fight, then Reg kicked Joe out and told him if he came back again he'd call the police.'

After Mrs Platt had gone Kate went in to Tom and told him what had happened.

'It's probably undone all the good that his therapy sessions have done,' remarked Kate bitterly.

'Maybe not,' said Tom thoughtfully. 'He may just get over it when he's had time to cool down. We'll see if he turns up tomorrow. If he does and he's still agitated I'll see about putting him back on his medication.'

'And if he doesn't turn up?'

'Then we'll go back to his lodgings — we'll contact him somehow, Kate, don't worry. You'll probably find he'll get over this in his own way.'

'I only hope you're right,' she said grimly, then glancing at her watch, she said. 'I'd better be getting home and organise some supper — I hope you like Italian food?'

'Love it,' he smiled. 'And it'll go with the bottle of Chianti I've bought.'

When she got home Kate set Nicola preparing a fresh fruit salad while she made the bolognese sauce and set the table. Beverley was the first to arrive, and the two girls were engaged in a heated argument about homework when the doorbell rang.

'Oh, it's him!' Nicola's hand flew to her mouth and she stared round-eyed at Beverley.

'Don't you think you should let him in?' asked Kate with a calmness she was far from feeling.

'But. . .'

'He's your guest.'

'Oh, all right.' Smoothing her hands down over the striped top she wore over her jeans, Nicola straightened her shoulders and headed for the front door.

Seconds later Kate heard Tom's voice and felt her knees weaken, and as she walked out of the kitchen her eyes met his across the lounge. In one hand he carried the bottle of Chianti and in the other a bunch of freesias.

'Hello, Kate.' He handed her the wine, then turning to Nicola he said, 'Some flowers for my hostess.'

Kate saw Nicola's cheeks grow pink, Beverley tittered, but Tom, completely unperturbed, separated the freesias, handing one bunch to Nicola, then turning back to Kate he said, 'And some for her mum. Hello, you must be Beverley—I'm Tom.'

He'd done it just right, thought Kate as she buried her nose in the freesias and hurried back to the kitchen to find vases. And if she'd worried that he might have been embarrassed by the two girls, that too was quickly dispelled, as throughout the meal he kept them enthralled with stories of America and, later, with eye witness accounts of Grand Prix racing.

It was as they were finishing the fruit salad that Kate suddenly said, 'I saw your friend today, Nicola—the one who spoke to you in the precinct that day. Kim, isn't it?'

As she mentioned Kim's name Kate was immediately aware of the glance that passed between her daughter and Beverley.

'Has she been ill?' Kate persisted when neither girl spoke.

'I don't think so. . . Why?' asked Nicola at last.

'Well, she wasn't at school, and it was in the middle of the day.'

'That's nothing new,' said Beverley darkly. 'She's off school more than she's there.'

Kate frowned. 'You did say she was in your year, didn't you?' She turned to her daughter, noticing the mulish expression on her features.

'Yes. Why?'

'She looks older than you two.'

'She is,' said Beverley. 'She's two years older. But she's been travelling around a lot with her family and she got behind with her schoolwork.'

'I'm not surprised, if she doesn't go to school even when she has the chance,' said Kate as she stood up and began collecting the plates. 'Would you like cheese and biscuits, Tom?'

'Do you mind if we go down to the video shop?' asked Nicola. 'They've got that new one in that we've been waiting for.'

'I don't like her,' said Beverley suddenly, and the others looked at her.

'You don't like who?' asked Kate.

'Kim,' said Beverley. 'I don't like Kim—she's weird.'

'I know you don't like her,' said Nicola, tossing her hair back from her face and standing up, 'but I do. Now, are you coming down the shop with me or not?'

'Well, what did you make of that?' Kate, the plates still in her hands, stared at Tom as the two girls disappeared.

'Bit of jealousy on Bev's part? Sounds as if her friendship with Nicola's been pretty exclusive until

now. She probably sees this girl Kim as some sort of
threat.'

'I hope she isn't,' said Kate slowly. 'A threat, I
mean,' she explained when Tom raised his eyebrows. 'There's something about this Kim that
makes me uneasy.' She shrugged then and carried
the plates into the kitchen.

It was after she'd set out the cheese board and
was spooning coffee into the percolator that she felt
Tom's arms go round her.

'Do you think I've been convincing, or will Nicola
suspect I've been here before?' he murmured, burying his face in the hollow of her neck.

She stiffened at the feel of him, then relaxed and
leaned against him, relishing the brief moment of
contact. 'I don't think she suspects anything,' she
said at last.

'I've been wanting to do this all evening.' He
turned her towards him and taking her face between
his hands he brought his lips down on hers.

Kate sighed and gave herself up to the luxury of
the moment, for if she was truthful, she too had
spent the evening longing for the same thing. The
cheese board and percolator forgotten, she wound
her arms around his neck, responding to his kiss
with a fervency which obviously delighted him and
aroused him even further.

Then, like forbidden lovers, as if any second they
might be discovered, their movements became more
urgent. Tom's hands moved over her body, mould-

ing the lines of her breasts and hips and encircling her waist.

'You're beautiful, Kate,' he whispered. 'You've been on my mind constantly—I can't stop thinking about that night. . . Kate, I want you now. . .'

'We can't, Tom, not now. . .'

'Please,' his voice was deep, husky with desire. 'I can't wait.'

'The girls will be back. . .they've only gone to. . .'

'Then when?' he demanded roughly in a tone that thrilled Kate to the core. 'Tomorrow? Tomorrow night? Come to my flat.'

'All right,' she whispered, then as the front door clicked she pulled sharply away from him.

Desperately she attempted to smooth her hair where Tom had tousled it, while he picked up the cheese board and calmly carried it through to the table. 'Hi, girls, what video did you get?' she heard him say.

Kate sighed and leaned weakly against the fridge. Why didn't she simply tell Nicola about herself and Tom and be done with all this deceit? She wasn't sure, however, that even she knew the answer to that. Was it because her daughter seemed to regard Tom Beresford as her own property? Or was it because she had agreed to a no-strings affair with him, which she knew would be over when he returned to the States, and she didn't want her daughter to know she had agreed to such a thing? Or maybe it was a mixture of both.

All Kate knew as she returned to the lounge was

that she found it difficult to meet her daughter's gaze and that she was having to battle with some very unfamiliar emotions.

Later, when the girls had gone off to Nicola's bedroom to watch their film and she and Tom sat quietly together drinking coffee, she looked across at him. 'Thank you for being so understanding over Nicola,' she said quietly.

He shrugged and smiled. 'It's nothing — teen years are always difficult and have to be handled carefully.'

'It's funny, but I've never thought of Nicola as being difficult before,' mused Kate.

'That's because she's been content to be your little girl. Now she's spreading her wings and trying to prove she's a woman — you're not used to that, and neither is she.'

'I'm beginning to think you should have been a psychotherapist,' said Kate ruefully.

Tom laughed. 'It's like anything else — if you're too close to something you simply fail to see it.'

Beverley stayed that night with Nicola, and after Tom had gone, Kate, as she was leaving the bathroom to go to bed, overheard the two girls talking in Nicola's bedroom.

'But I was right about him being dishy, wasn't I?' she heard Nicola say.

'Yes. . .' said Beverley.

'You don't sound too sure.'

Kate paused, holding her breath.

'Well. . .he is nice, I agree, but don't you think. . .don't you think he's a bit old for you?'

'He's only thirty!'

'How do you know?'

'I asked him. Anyway, lots of women are attracted to older men.'

'I know.' Beverley still sounded doubtful. 'But have you thought, Nick, when you're thirty, he'll be . . .he'll be forty-seven!' Her voice rose incredulously, as if no one could even contemplate being forty-seven.

The two girls dissolved into giggles, and Kate stole silently away to her bedroom.

CHAPTER SEVEN

KATE'S first client the following morning was Stephanie, the woman who had left her husband. She was still tearful, and Kate knew she was badly missing her two children. The man she was living with was proving to be difficult and uncooperative, and Stephanie was rapidly reaching the point of discovering for herself that she might have made a serious mistake.

'Are you suggesting I go back to Mike?' she demanded almost angrily of Kate.

'I'm not suggesting anything, it's for you to decide,' answered Kate calmly.

'Mike's so boring, our relationship was dead — Gerry makes me feel alive again, makes me feel like a woman instead of just a mother and a house-wife.'

'Did Mike make you feel that way once?' asked Kate quietly. Stephanie looked up sharply and Kate noticed her eyes were bloodshot. 'Mike? Well, yes, I suppose he did once, but that was a very long time ago — it all changed.'

'What do you think changed it?'

Stephanie shrugged and lit a cigarette, drawing heavily, then exhaling. 'Things in general, I suppose — I don't know, you tell me, you're the expert.'

She paused, reflecting, then said, 'Having the kids changed things, I suppose.'

Kate was silent for a while, allowing Stephanie time to think then casually she said, 'And now it's the children who are changing your relationship with Gerry?'

'What do you mean?' Stephanie demanded, frowning.

'Well, it's pretty obvious that your worry over your children is having an effect on your life with Gerry.'

'Damn kids, I wish I'd never had them.' Stephanie angrily ground out her half-finished cigarette in the ashtray on Kate's desk, then when Kate remained silent, her shoulders slumped and she said wearily, 'I didn't mean that.'

'I know you didn't—if you didn't care you wouldn't be here.'

'So what am I going to do?' Helplessly Stephanie stared at Kate. 'Can't you tell me what to do?'

Kate shook her head. 'No, Stephanie, I'm not here to tell you what to do. I'm here to help you to explore your options so that you can make up your own mind.'

'I can't leave Gerry. I've never felt like this before, but maybe you don't know what I mean.'

When, ten minutes later, Kate watched Stephanie leave her room at the end of the session, she found herself thinking that she knew exactly what she meant, for she too was realising that Tom Beresford was making her feel like she never had before.

She glanced at her watch and saw that it was

almost time for Joe's session. She flicked the switch on her intercom and spoke to Julie, but the receptionist told her that Joe hadn't arrived.

Kate sighed. 'Thanks, Julie, if he does come will you send him up, please. Oh, Julie, is there anyone else for me to see?'

'No, Kate, no one else until eleven o'clock.'

Kate picked up the paper-knife from her desk and began opening her mail. It looked as if Joe wasn't going to turn up. She would have to ask Tom to visit his home again, and this time they would have to make some sort of contact.

Fifteen minutes later there was still no sign of Joe, and Kate slipped downstairs to the cloakroom. On her way back to her room as she passed Tom's door, he must have seen her, for he called out.

She put her head round the door and smiled at him.

'Thanks for last night,' he said softly.

'Sorry about the fan club,' she grinned.

'Don't mention it. I'm flattered to be the centre of so much female attention. I could get to like it.'

'Chauvinist!' she laughed, and would have carried on along the corridor, but he called her back.

'Kate, will you be able to get away tonight?'

She pursed her lips as if considering, then laughed and said, 'I'll see what I can do — Nicola's going to the youth club with Bev, so I should be free for a couple of hours at least. There's just one problem, I don't know where you live.'

'Marlborough Terrace — number twenty, flat six. Come for a meal.'

Kate was humming happily as she left Tom's room and climbed the stairs to her own room on the first floor, and when she found her door locked, at first she was puzzled. She rattled the handle, wondering for a moment if it had simply jammed when she had closed it, but it was definitely locked. She frowned and stood back, gazing at the closed door, then stepping forward again she knocked smartly, rattled the handle again and called out, but there wasn't a sound from inside the room. She glanced along the corridor; there was only the staff-room, store-room and kitchen on this floor besides her own room, and at this time of the morning it was deserted.

Still puzzled, Kate turned and ran lightly down the stairs again, along the corridor and into Reception. Julie and Lynn were on duty, and they both looked up in surprise.

'My consulting-room door's locked,' said Kate, aware how stupid that must sound. 'I came downstairs for a few minutes and when I got back it was locked. Do we have a spare key?'

Julie stared at her. 'Where's Joe?' she asked.

'Joe?' Kate frowned. 'He didn't turn up.'

'Yes, he did. He was late, but I sent him up to you like you asked.'

Kate stood very still for a moment, then she said, 'Does Dr Beresford have a patient?'

'Yes, one has just gone in,' replied Lynn, then, her eyes widening, she said, 'You don't think Joe has locked himself in your room?'

'It sounds like it,' agreed Kate.

'Dr Rayner doesn't have a patient at the moment,' said Julie.

'Right, thanks, Julie.' Kate hurried from Reception and tapped urgently on Bernard Rayner's door.

Moments later she and Bernard were running up the stairs to the first floor. They found the door still locked, but this time faint sounds could be heard from inside.

'Joe,' Kate called. 'Joe, can you hear me? It's Kate. Will you open the door for me?'

The sounds from within ceased, and Kate looked at Bernard.

'Try again,' he said softly. 'He knows you, it may upset him if he hears my voice.'

'Joe, please let me in,' called Kate. 'I thought we were going to have a talk this morning. I can't talk to you very well through the door.'

Joe's silence continued as for the next fifteen minutes Kate tried to persuade him to open the door. While she talked she and Bernard were joined first by Tom, then Malcolm, who suggested they might have to call the police.

'I wouldn't have thought that would be necessary, from what Kate has told me and from his records,' said Tom quietly. 'He doesn't have a previous history of violence, does he, Kate?'

She shook her head. 'Not really. The only time he seems to have retaliated is against his stepfather.'

'But is he likely to harm himself?' asked Malcom.

'That of course is always a possibility, especially in his present frame of mind,' said Kate.

'I don't think we need the police,' said Bernard, 'but I think we should force the door.'

'I'll do it,' Tom stood back. 'Are you ready?' He glanced at the others, and when they nodded he put his shoulder to the door. It gave way at the second attempt and burst open.

The sight which met their eyes seemed momentarily to paralyse them, for it looked as if a snowstorm had hit Kate's room.

Kate gasped and stood still, gaping at the white-covered desk, carpet and chairs.

Joe was crouched in the corner by the window, his hands over his head. Kate's paper-knife lay on the carpet in front of him, together with the remains of her patchwork cushions, which had been ripped to shreds. And it was in that split second that she realised that it was feathers that covered the room, floating in the air and sticking to every surface.

While Bernard retrieved the paper-knife, Tom and Malcolm helped Joe to his feet. His dark eyes looked enormous in his thin face and his hair was matted and uncombed. For a moment he looked wild and frightened, then his gaze found Kate.

'It's all right, Joe,' she said softly. 'No one's going to hurt you.' Then helplessly she watched as Tom led him away, presumably to his own consulting-room.

When she bent down to pick up one of the tattered

cushions she found she had a lump in her throat, and tears pricked the back of her eyes.

Julie helped Kate to clean up her room, but it was lunchtime before Kate joined the doctors in the staff-room and learnt that Joe had been admitted to hospital.

'He was more disturbed than I thought,' said Tom. 'I rang the consultant psychiatrist who'd previously treated Joe, and he suggested he saw him. A social worker took him to the hospital, but there was no need to section him—he was admitted quite voluntarily.'

'Poor Joe,' said Kate, 'I'd thought I was getting somewhere with him—we really seemed to be getting to the root of his problems—but this business over the cushion and his mother's birthday seemed to tip the balance.'

'Yes, and the fact that, as you've just said, your therapy sessions were getting close to his problem—maybe too many memories had been churned up just recently.'

Kate glanced sharply at Tom. 'Are you blaming psychotherapy again?'

Tom shrugged. 'Not necessarily. I was simply giving a point of view.'

'I hope you two aren't going to squabble,' said Bernard with a sigh. 'There's been enough drama round here this morning without you adding to it.'

Kate laughed. 'It's all right, Bernard, don't

worry—it's just that Tom and I sometimes dispute the value of therapy, that's all.'

'That's all right, then,' muttered Bernard, 'we don't want anyone falling out.' He strode out of the staff-room to start on his morning house calls, and as Kate watched him go she wondered what he would say if he knew the real relationship between herself and Tom.

Almost as if he could read her thoughts Tom looked at her raised eyebrows. 'I have antenatal clinic this afternoon, but I'll see you later. What time will you be able to come over?'

She hesitated, then said, 'About seven-thirty?'

He nodded, and at the expression in his eyes her heart seemed to turn over, then he too turned and left the room.

Kate found difficulty in concentrating for the rest of the day, as the episode with Joe had upset her more than she cared to admit, and she was also wondering what she was going to say to Nicola about going out that evening. She didn't want to tell her daughter a direct lie, but neither did she want her to suspect the truth. By the time she got home she was on edge and jumpy, and when Nicola came home from Bev's where she had been doing her homework Kate had to pretend she had already eaten.

'Why didn't you wait?' asked Nicola, tucking into the salad Kate had prepared for her.

'Because I have to go out.'

'Oh?' Nicola glanced up. It was rare for Kate to go out unless the trip included them both.

'Yes—something to do with work,' Kate mumbled, and turned to the sink. She had on occasions seen clients in the evenings, and she hoped that Nicola would think just that. 'You're going to the youth club, aren't you?' she asked when her daughter remained silent.

'Yes, I suppose so.'

'Why do you say it like that?' Kate turned from the sink in surprise. 'I thought you liked the youth club.'

Nicola sighed and pushed her plate away. 'It's got so boring lately. . . I may stay the night at Bev's,' she added.

Kate stood very still and stared down at the soapsuds in the sink. Did this mean she and Tom could spend another night together? 'So how will I know?' she asked, hoping her voice sounded casual.

'Know what?' Nicola bit into an apple.

'Whether you'll be coming home or not.'

Nicola was silent for a moment, and when Kate turned again she found her staring at her. 'I'll phone,' she said at last, then added, 'like I always do.'

'Oh, yes, all right,' said Kate faintly, then as she watched her daughter leave the table and disappear to her room, she wondered yet again why she didn't just tell her about herself and Tom. In some respects it would make life a lot easier, but still she hesitated. Nicola would be upset, she knew that, and was it really worth it for a relationship that was going to be so shortlived?

Kate knew Marlborough Terrace, it was on the far side of town, a curved row of Regency town houses, which like those in Cromwell Road had all been converted into flats and apartments. But there the similarity ended, for the houses in Marlborough Terrace had lost none of their charm or elegance in their conversion. It was another warm summer's evening, and as Kate brought her car to a halt outside Number Twenty there was barely a breath of wind to stir the branches of the lime trees that fringed the avenue.

She took a moment to look up at the white façade of the houses with their black balconies, the shiny front doors flanked by iron railings and tubs of bright geraniums, and at the same time she tried to control the racing of her pulse. She felt like a young girl on her first date, her throat dry with anticipation, her nerves stretched to breaking point and the blood pounding in her head.

Then she was ringing the bell of Flat Six and Tom's voice was telling her to come up, and seconds later he was there, before her. With a little sound between a sob and a laugh she went straight into his arms.

'At last!' he murmured between kisses. 'I couldn't bear it much longer, this seeing you, being with you but forbidden to touch. . . Ah, Kate, what have you done to me?'

They made love immediately, and although it lacked none of the spontaneity of the last time, this time it also held the added thrill of planned anticipation. This time Tom undressed her, carefully, deliberately, delighting in her soft skin and the smooth curtain of her hair as he released it from its bow and it tumbled about her shoulders.

Briefly, momentarily she agonised that he might find her unattractive, that the age difference between them might bother him, that he might be used to making love to nubile young girls with taut, firm flesh, girls who had never had a child. . .then the thought was gone as once again she gave herself up to the exquisite excitement of his caresses.

Then a little later, as he began to take her towards that peak of pleasure she had known before with him, Kate's thoughts wandered briefly and again she found herself in sympathy with Stephanie, for like her and the way she felt for Gerry, she too had never felt this way before, just as she also knew she would find this virtually impossible to give up.

Much later, as she lay satiated in Tom's arms, he began curling strands of her hair around his fingers. 'That wasn't the way I'd planned things at all,' he said solemnly.

'What do you mean?' Lazily she lifted her head to look at him, loving the strong firm lines of his profile and the beautifully chiselled shape of his lips.

'I'd decided we'd be very civilised.'

'Whatever for?' she laughed wickedly.

'I'd planned drinks when you arrived, then a leisurely meal followed by coffee and intellient conversation — why, I even had the music ready — *La Bohème*, and the flowers. . .but then you arrived and you stood there in your flowery dress looking utterly enchanting, and I wanted you so much, all my good intentions flew out of the window.'

'Oh, Tom!' Kate was laughing now at his contrite expression. 'Are you trying to tell me that this wasn't on your original agenda?'

'Of course not!' He looked shocked. 'You don't ask a lady to your flat with this in mind.'

'Oh, of course not.'

'Mind you,' he said after a moment's pause during which Kate once again lovingly examined his features, 'if it happens. . .'

They both dissolved into laughter which preceded more loving, and it was much later when they finally sipped the Buck's Fizz that Tom had planned as the prelude to their evening. But it was later than that, after they had eaten, and while they lingered over coffee, that Tom said wistfully, 'Can't you stay the night?'

His tone of voice suggested that he expected her refusal, and when she hesitated, he looked up in surprise.

'I'm not sure,' she said slowly, and when he raised his eyebrows she went on to explain, 'Nicola may be staying the night at Bev's, but she wasn't certain. She said she'd phone and let me know.'

'Doesn't she know you were going out?' A glint of amusement came into his eyes.

'Yes, but she thinks I'm with a client. . .she wouldn't expect me to be too long. I think I'll have to get home soon, Tom, so I'll be there if she phones.'

'And if she does phone and says she's not coming home? What'll you do then?'

'What do you mean?' She met his amused stare and her pulses began to race again.

'Will you stay there on your own, or will you come back here and spend the night with me?'

'I. . . I don't know. . .' She hesitated, hating herself for her uncharacteristic indecision.

'Tell you what,' he drained his cup and stood up, 'I have a better idea. Why not phone Nicola at Bev's? Say you've been delayed, that you might be late and that you were concerned about her.'

Still she hesitated, but then Tom reached out his hand and drawing her to her feet pulled her towards him, enfolding her in his arms. And as she caught the citrus scent of his aftershave mingling with his own male aroma, reminding her momentarily of the passion they had shared earlier, she knew she wanted to stay the night with him, just as the tautening and hardening of his body told her that was exactly what he wanted. His kiss was rough, demanding, then, holding her away from him, his eyes hungrily raking her face, he said huskily, 'The phone's through there.'

Without another word she pulled away from him and hurried to the kitchen.

Bev's was one of the numbers Kate knew from memory, and while the phone was ringing at the other end and she waited for someone to answer, she realised her heart was thumping. Bev's mother finally answered the phone.

'Oh, hello, Janice, it's Kate Riley here. Is Nicola still with you?'

'Hello, Kate. No, I'm sorry, Nicola's not here. Would you like to speak to Bev? Maybe she'll know where she is. I'll just get her for you.'

Kate felt a stab of disappointment. It sounded as if her daughter was on her way home, and if that was the case she would have to put all thoughts of spending the night with Tom firmly out of her mind. 'Oh, hello, Bev,' she said as she heard the girl's voice.

'Hello, Mrs Riley.'

'Bev, I was ringing to see if Nicola was still there, but your mother said she wasn't. Has she been gone long?'

There was a silence at the other end of the line.

'Nicola told me she might have been going to spend the night with you, and I was just ringing to find out. . . Bev? Hello? Are you still there?'

'Yes, Mrs Riley. . .um, no, Nicola isn't spending the night here.'

'Bev, did you go to the youth club with Nicola tonight?' asked Kate.

'Er. . .did she say she was going to the youth club?'

'Yes, she did,' said Kate, then when there was yet another silence from the other end of the line, taking a deep breath, she said, 'It's all right, Bev, I won't ask you to grass on her.'

After she'd hung up she stood for a moment staring at the phone. If her daughter wasn't with Bev then where was she? Hearing a slight sound behind her, she turned sharply and found Tom lounging in the doorway.

'Well?' he said lazily. 'Can you stay?'

Kate shook her head. 'No, Tom, I'm afraid I can't.'

His face dropped. 'Nicola not staying at Bev's?'

'No. And not only is she not staying there, she hasn't even been there this evening, neither has she been to the youth club. I shall have to go home, Tom. It looks as if my daughter's been deceiving me.'

CHAPTER EIGHT

THE house was empty when Kate got home, and she felt the first twinge of alarm. It was so unlike Nicola to go anywhere without telling her—in fact, it was the strictest rule that Kate laid down, that she always knew where Nicola was going and with whom.

It was a full half-hour before the phone rang, and by that time Kate, after working herself up into a state and picturing her daughter lying on waste ground somewhere having been raped and probably murdered, was on the verge of ringing the police.

She snatched up the receiver. 'Hello?' she shouted.

'Mum? Where have you been? I tried to ring before.'

'Nicola, where are you?'

'Mum, I think I'll stay after all.'

'Stay where, Nicola?' Kate was aware her voice had risen an octave.

'You know. . . I told you——'

'You told me you were with Bev, but you aren't, are you?'

There was a silence, then Kate heard her daughter sigh. 'No, I'm not with Bev.'

'Then where are you, for heaven's sake?'

'I'm at Kim's,' said Nicola.

'Kim!' An image of the red-haired girl in her black flowing clothes flitted through Kate's mind.

'Yes. I thought I'd stay——'

'I'll be over to pick you up right away,' said Kate sharply, replacing the receiver with a bang.

Nicola was waiting on the pavement outside the house in Cromwell Road when Kate brought the car to an abrupt halt. There was no sign of Kim. Kate leaned across and unlocked the passenger door, Nicola got in and fastened her safety-belt, and without a word Kate drove away.

The silence continued until they were almost home, then Kate threw a glance at her daughter. Her face was set, her expression mutinous, and she stared straight ahead.

'Why didn't you tell me you were going there?' asked Kate at last.

Nicola sighed and rolled her eyes, but remained silent.

'Nicola, I want an answer.' Kate tried to keep her voice calm, knowing she had to handle this carefully.

'Would you have let me go, if I'd said?' There was a contemptuous note in her daughter's voice, and when Kate hesitated, Nicola went on, 'You wouldn't would you? I knew you wouldn't, that's why I didn't ask.'

'But if you knew I wouldn't let you go, you must also have known I would have had a good reason.' Kate gave an exasperated sigh as she drew the car into their garage. Switching off the ignition, she

rested her hands on the steering-wheel and turned
to her daughter. 'For God's sake, Nicola, I thought
we had an understanding — you never go anywhere
unless you tell me. I thought you'd gone to the youth
club tonight, then back to Bev's.'

'I'm thirteen, Mum! Not ten!' Nicola threw Kate
a withering look. 'And I'm bored with the youth
club — I'd much rather go to Kim's club.'

'What do you mean, Kim's club?' Kate frowned.

By this time Nicola was climbing out of the car,
and it wasn't until Kate had followed her to the front
door that she answered. 'Oh, it's just some friends
that meet at Kim's house.'

'Are they people from school?' Kate pushed open
the door and realised the phone was ringing.

'Some of them are,' said Nicola airily, and ran up
the stairs, leaving Kate to answer the phone.

Wearily she lifted the receiver, then as she heard
Tom's voice her heart skipped a beat.

'Is everything all right? I've been trying to reach
you for the past half-hour.'

'Oh, yes, thank you, everything's OK now,' she
said weakly, sinking down on to the stairs as she
spoke. Suddenly she felt very tired, but at the same
time comforted by the sound of Tom's voice, pleased
that he had shown concern when he could have
simply been irritated by her abrupt departure.

'Is Nicola home?' he asked.

'Yes, she is now. I've just picked her up. She was
at another girl's house, not Bev's.'

'I see. Well, just so long as she's OK. Kate?'

'Yes?'

'Don't be too hard on her.'

Kate continued to sit on the stairs for some while after she had hung up, then at a sound from above she glanced round. Nicola was leaning over the banisters.

'Who was that on the phone?' she asked, and Kate thought she detected a suspicious note in her voice.

She only hesitated for a moment. 'Tom Beresford.'

'Tom? But I heard you say you'd picked me up from another girl's house, not Bev's.'

'That's right, I did,' replied Kate, playing for time as she tried to think of a suitable explanation as to why Tom should have phoned.

'But how did he know?' There was an accusing frown on Nicola's face now.

Kate sighed. 'I told you I had to go out this evening and it was concerned with work.'

'And Tom was there?'

'He was.'

'Why?' Nicola demanded.

'You know better than to ask me that, Nicola. I've told you before, my work is totally confidential.'

Her daughter continued to stare at her for a moment, then turned and flounced away to her room. Kate took a deep breath, then went through to the kitchen and filled the kettle.

She needed time to think, and she carried her mug

of coffee out on to the tiny patio at the back of the house, sat down on a bench and leaning back against the wall briefly closed her eyes.

She knew she had to handle this situation with her daughter very carefully—she sighed as she thought of the many times her clients had described similar problems to her, and she found herself trying to imagine how she would react in those circumstances, but it was impossible. It was very different when it was your own problem and it was much more difficult to be rational. She still felt angry with Nicola, and she tried to analyse the cause of her anger. Was it because this was the first time to her knowledge that Nicola had deceived her, or was it because what had happened had prevented her from spending the night with Tom? They had always been straight and truthful with each other in the past— then with a pang Kate realised that if her daughter had deceived her by going to Kim's, then she in turn had deceived Nicola.

Restlessly she stirred, unwilling to accept that the situations were the same. Nicola was only thirteen years old and needed protection, and hadn't she only kept the truth about herself and Tom from Nicola to prevent her being hurt? So why hadn't Nicola told her the truth? She had implied that if Kate had known she wanted to go to Kim's, she would have stopped her. What was it about Kim that made Nicola so certain her mother would disapprove?

Kate opened her eyes, finished her coffee, then stood up and glanced up at her daughter's bedroom window. There was only one way to find out, and purposefully she made her way back into the house.

Nicola was lying on her bed watching her television, her arms round her pink hippo. She eyed her mother warily as Kate came into the room and sat on the side of the bed.

'Nicky, we need to talk,' said Kate.

'What about?'

'About you being friends with Kim. Do you think we could have the telly off for a while?'

Nicola switched off the set with the remote control, then stared at Kate. 'I don't think you would approve of Kim,' she said flatly.

'Why do you think that?'

Nicola shrugged, pushing the hair back out of her eyes. 'I don't know really—she's just not like us.'

'Her family, you mean?' queried Kate.

Nicola nodded. 'Yes, I suppose so. They're different, but I just don't think you'd like the way they live.'

'Don't you think it might be a good idea to give me the chance to find out?' asked Kate.

'What do you mean?' Nicola stared at her.

'Well, why don't you bring Kim home so that I can meet her properly?'

'Bring Kim here?' echoed Nicola.

'Yes, why not?'

'I don't know,' Nicola muttered, and shifted restlessly on her bed. 'I'm not sure. . .'

'Look, Nicky, can't we reach an agreement on this? If you want to carry on a friendship with Kim you bring her here first so that I can meet her — surely that's reasonable? I won't eat her!' Kate laughed. 'Come on, Nicky, we've always managed to work things out before, haven't we? Is it a deal?'

At last, grudgingly, Nicola nodded, and Kate breathed a sigh of relief. There was still something about this girl Kim that made her uneasy, but at least if she were to meet her and talk to her it might help to put her mind at rest.

The following morning after Nicola had left for school and Kate was almost ready for work, Lottie arrived, and Kate stayed for a moment to ask how she was feeling.

'Them tablets Dr Beresford gave me are marvellous,' said Lottie as she fastened her overall. 'I don't keep having to run to the loo every five minutes like I did before.'

'That's good. What about your diet?' asked Kate.

'I can't say that's a bundle of fun. . . I don't like that bran stuff he said I have to sprinkle over things, and I can't say I'm too partial to that wholemeal bread either — I've always liked a nice crusty white loaf myself — the veg isn't a problem, though, I've always been one for my vegetables.'

'Well, you just persevere, Lottie,' said Kate. 'I'm sure you'll be as right as rain again in no time. Have you had your appointment yet for your X-ray?'

'No, not yet. Can't say as how I'm looking forward to that,' sniffed Lottie.

'Let me know when it is, and if I can, I'll run you up to the hospital,' Kate told her.

'That's very kind of you, Mrs Riley. I've to see Dr Beresford again afterwards — talking of him, how long is he here for?'

'Only until Dr Scott gets back.'

'That's a pity — he's a nice man.' said Lottie.

Kate let herself out of the house, smiling at how Lottie seemed to have changed her opinion of Tom.

He was waiting for her when she drove into the car park, and her heart skipped a beat at the sight of him. As she switched off the engine he leaned through the open window of her car. 'Is everything all right?' he asked softly.

'I think so. . .thanks for phoning last night.'

'I wondered whether I should or not. Did Nicola comment on it?'

'She did. I'm afraid my daughter doesn't miss much, but I was able to pass it off by implying that we'd been together because of work.'

'You still don't think it would be easier to tell her?' he asked as he held the door open for her.

'No, Tom, I don't think so. I know it would upset her, and even if she did accept it, you'd be gone just as she'd be getting used to having you around.'

He didn't answer, and when she glanced at him she saw he had a tight expression on his features. 'Besides,' she went on quickly, 'I think my daughter is going through a difficult time anyway with her own relationships, without us adding to her problems.'

'Who was she with last night?' Tom asked as they made their way into the health centre.

'That girl Kim,' answered Kate grimly.

'And you obviously don't approve?'

'I'm uneasy about it, but I'm not really in a position to disapprove, because I don't know the girl. But Nicola and I have reached the understanding that if she wants to be friends with her she brings her home so that at least I can meet her. It's funny, Tom, but when Nicola's with Bev I still think of her as a child, but there've been times lately when she's seemed almost adult, and as for that girl Kim — well, she looks years older than Nicola.'

'You know Malcolm's been having similar worries over his son Theo?' queried Tom.

'Yes, He did mention something the other day — truancy, wasn't it?'

Tom nodded. 'Apparently a group of them were caught smoking pot.'

'Oh, dear, poor Malcolm!' said Kate feelingly.

'Is Theo at the same school as Nicola?'

'Yes, although he's a bit older,' replied Kate, suddenly comforted that she wasn't the only one having problems. They paused for a moment at the foot of the stairs, and Kate, changing the subject, said, 'I saw Lottie this morning.'

'How is she?' asked Tom.

'She said the tablets were making her feel a lot better — and Tom, I think you've got another recruit for your fan club!'

'Whatever do you mean?' he queried.

She smiled as he looked embarrassed. 'Well, Lottie seems to have gone from not wanting to see a male doctor in any circumstances, to not wanting you to go away.' She smiled up at him as she spoke, and as he looked down into her eyes she was reminded of the intensity of their lovemaking the evening before, and Kate knew that she too was rapidly reaching the point where she didn't want him to go away, in spite of the fact that she had believed she didn't want any long-term commitment.

He took a step towards her, and for one wild moment she thought he was going to kiss her. His mouth was only inches from hers, and she caught her breath in sudden anticipation, then the front door clicked and Bernard walked in.

They sprang apart, but were both aware of the strange look the senior partner gave them as he muttered an abrupt good morning and strode down the corridor to his room.

'I think it's time we did some work, Mrs Riley,' said Tom softly, 'before we get ourselves talked about — but before you go, when do I get to see you again?'

'I'm not sure, Tom,' she hesitated. 'I suppose it'll be at Bernard and Sue's party at the end of the week.'

A smile touched his mouth, and Kate found herself longing for him to take her in his arms and kiss her and to hell with the rest of the staff.

'Much as I like Bernard and Sue, that isn't quite what I had in mind,' he said, then with a wink he was gone, leaving Kate in no doubt whatsoever just what it was he had in mind.

* * *

Kate was kept extremely busy for the rest of the week with several new referrals, including one from Tom for bereavement counselling for a woman who had lost her husband suddenly in a road accident and was finding it difficult coming to terms with her loss. She was both surprised and pleased that Tom had referred one of his patients, for she had doubted that he would after the conversations they had had concerning her work.

She had a further session with Stephanie, who still remained very confused over what she should do, and she had two further sessions with the young man suffering from claustrophobia. With him, Kate felt she was at last making some headway.

At home Kate was relieved that things seemed to have returned to normal between herself and her daughter. Nicola hadn't suggested bringing Kim home, in fact the older girl's name hadn't been mentioned again, and Nicola seemed content with Bev's company once more.

On Saturday morning, as Kate was catching up on some chores and Nicola was finishing her homework, the phone rang.

'I'll get it!' called Nicola, and Kate carried on with folding clean clothes and packing them into the airing cupboard. When her daughter didn't call her she guessed the call must have been for her. Kate felt happy that morning and was looking forward to the Rayners' party. It might be a very public affair, and she knew she would have to be careful, but at least she would see Tom and be able to spend some time in his company. She paused for a moment, then buried her face in the soft scented pile of some clean towels. Tom was occupying more and more of her thoughts these days, and she found that when she wasn't with him she constantly counted the hours until she knew she would see him again. Then she turned sharply as Nicola bounded up the stairs; there was a broad grin on her daughter's face.

'Guess who that was,' she said.

For a second Kate's heart sank as she thought it might have been Kim. 'I don't know. Who?'

'Tom!' said Nicola triumphantly.

'Tom?' Kate heard herself say faintly. 'What did he want?'

'He rang to see if we wanted to go motor racing at the end of the month.'

'We?' asked Kate tentatively.

'Yes, he said you could come as well, if you want.'

'Oh, what did you say?'

'I said yes, of course.' Nicola stared at Kate incredulously, then she said, 'You needn't come if you don't want to, but I shall go.'

Kate swallowed. 'Of course I'll go, it was very kind of Tom to ask us.'

'Yes,' Nicola smiled in a satisfied sort of way. 'Wait till I tell Bev!' she said, and turned to go into her bedroom, then she paused and looked back. 'Oh, there was just one other thing—Tom said he'd pick us up tonight to go to the Rayners'. I must go and find something to wear.' She disappeared into her room, and it was Kate's turn to smile.

Tom picked them up just after seven, and Kate read the silent admiration in his eyes when he saw the loose olive-green trousers and cream silk shirt she'd chosen to wear, but he cleverly voiced his approval of Nicola's choice of patterned ski-pants and baggy scarlet shirt fastened with a huge buckled belt that sat neatly on her slim hips.

Bernard and Susan Rayner lived on the outskirts of West Chillerton in a large old property that had once been a manor. The house with its twisted chimneys and mellow red brick was believed to be late Elizabethan, while its large garden, thick with shrubbery and herbacious borders, sported a brick pergola tumbling with cream roses.

They were not the first to arrive, and after they had been greeted by the Rayners they carried drinks outside, where they found a game of croquet in full swing on the large lawns at the rear of the house. The Rayners' two children, Sophie and Charles, and Malcolm's son Theo, immediately drew Nicola into the game, and Kate and Tom wandered through the pergola and found a seat at the far end against a neatly clipped yew hedge.

'Fantastic place Bernard has,' remarked Tom as they sat down and looked back towards the house. The evening sun had turned the brickwork a soft rose and was glinting on several of the hundreds of tiny panes in the latticed windows.

'Yes, it's beautiful,' agreed Kate. 'So peaceful—I always feel I've stepped back into the past when I come here. Mind you, it wasn't always like this—it was almost derelict when Bernard and Susan took it over. They've literally restored it to its former glory.'

'It must have cost a fortune to do,' observed Tom thoughtfully.

'Apparently it did,' said Kate. 'My sister told me that Susan had a large legacy from an aunt, and it all went on restoring the house.'

'Well, it's a wonderful investment. I love anything like this, in fact the only thing I miss about living in the States is the lack of really old buildings and the sense of history.'

They fell silent, and Kate stole a glance at Tom. What he had just said had reminded her that soon he would be going — out of her life again, probably forever. But that had been what they had agreed, what they had both wanted. And it was still what she wanted. Wasn't it? She stirred restlessly and looked up at the thick cream roses that cascaded over the wooden beams of the pergola, and quite suddenly she envied the Rayners living in this beautiful house which they had so lovingly restored and bringing up their family, and deep inside her she felt an emptiness, a deep sense of loss, as if there was something vital missing from her own life.

'Nicola seems happy here,' observed Tom almost as if he could read her thoughts as he nodded towards the lawns, where from time to time they caught glimpses of Nicola's scarlet shirt as she darted across the grass with her mallet.

'Yes, she loves it here,' admitted Kate, then

added, 'Thank you for asking us to the motor racing—she was thrilled about that.'

'Don't mention it, it'll be a pleasure. How have things been the last few days?' asked Tom.

'Much better. She hasn't mentioned Kim again. I hope things are back to normal now.' Kate glanced up quickly as something suddenly caught her eye. 'Oh, it looks as if Fran has arrived with her tribe,' she said, then standing up she looked down at Tom and added, 'Come on, come and meet my sister.'

CHAPTER NINE

Much later, after they had eaten some of the delicious Stroganoff and rice that Susan had cooked, Kate sat with her sister on the steps that led from the terrace to the lawns, watching the croquet. The young people had now been joined by some of the men, including Tom and Fran's husband Ron, and the frequent crack of mallet on woods mingled with their laughter and hung in the still evening air.

Idly Kate snapped a piece of lavender from a bush beside the steps, crushed the deep blue flowers between her fingers and sniffed the fragrance, inhaling deeply and briefly closing her eyes.

'He looks like Brian,' said Fran suddenly, and Kate's eyes snapped open.

'I beg your pardon.' She glanced sharply at her sister.

'Your friend,' Fran nodded towards the lawn where Tom was retrieving his wood from the longer grass beneath a clump of hydrangeas. 'I noticed the moment I met him — he's the image of Brian.'

Kate remained silent, suddenly amazed as she realised that since she had got to know Tom better she had in fact forgotten his resemblance to Brian. Fran threw her a quick glance. 'Don't tell me you didn't notice, because I won't believe you.'

'Of course I noticed,' said Kate tersely, then added, 'But he's not a bit like Brian when you get to know him.'

'I'm relieved to hear it,' said Fran drily. 'But was it that that first attracted you to him?'

'Whatever do you mean?' Kate tried to sound indignant.

'Come off it, Kate!' Fran laughed out loud. 'It's me, your sister, you're talking to, and you don't fool me for one moment — you're head over heels in love with him.'

'I. . . I. . .don't. . .'

'And he is with you,' concluded Fran. 'It stands out a mile — you've only got to see the way he looks at you. What does Nicola think about it?'

'Nicola doesn't know,' said Kate quietly, shocked that it had taken her sister to make her see the truth, that she really was in love with Tom. But whether Fran was right about Tom being in love with her or not, she wasn't too sure.

'She seems to be getting on well with him,' observed Fran. 'When are you going to tell her?'

'There's nothing to tell,' said Kate quickly, afraid suddenly that her sister, having jumped to the right conclusions, would say too much. 'Tom's going back to the States to live very shortly — we both agreed to a brief affair, but that's all. When he goes it'll be over.'

'Pity,' said Fran, standing up and smoothing down her dress. 'He seems nice, and it's about time you thought about settling down again.'

Yes, thought Kate as she watched her sister walk back to the house, he is nice, very nice — and yes, it would be rather nice to settle down again. Then she shook herself. Whatever was she thinking about? She valued her independence, she loved her career and she was perfectly content with the life she and Nicola lived; they were quite happy, they didn't need anyone else.

She was about to follow her sister into the house when Malcolm Symonds suddenly joined her. 'Kate, could I have a quiet word?' he said, sitting down beside her.

'Of course. What is it, Malcolm?'

'No doubt you'll have heard, we've been having some problems with Theo recently.' He pulled a face, and Kate nodded sympathetically.

'Yes, I did hear something,' she said. 'Is everything OK now?'

'I hope so, but I was wondering whether some counselling might help him.'

'You mean for him to come to me?' Kate sounded doubtful, and Malcolm glanced at her.

'You would object?'

'I wouldn't object, but I wonder whether Theo would want to talk to me.'

'I think he might — he likes you, Kate.'

'Well, I'd certainly be willing to try if you'd think it would help.'

'Jill and I have tried to talk to him, obviously, but he just clams up — you know how it is. The main problem seems to be with the crowd he's got in with at school. Jenkins, the headmaster, nearly flipped when he heard about the pot-smoking — he was quite convinced he didn't have a drug problem at his school.'

'Was it happening on the premises?' asked Kate, noticing as she spoke that Nicola had detached herself from the group on the lawn and was walking towards them.

'No, they were caught in a raid in a house in Cromwell Road, but all the children concerned were pupils at the school, my son included,' said Malcolm grimly.

There it was again — Cromwell Road, thought Kate uneasily, then she dismissed the thought as Malcolm's pager went off at the precise moment that Nicola reached the steps.

'Mum, can I stay the night with Sophie and Charles?' Nicola asked eagerly as Malcolm hurried off into the house to find a telephone, then, seeing Kate's expression, she added pointedly, 'It's all right, their mother said I could.'

A little later they all moved into the house, the young people disappeared upstairs to play music, while the adults sat in the drawing-room or the oak panelled hall and talked. Like Kate, Susan Rayner was passionately fond of opera, and the sound of well-known arias drifted through the house and over the twilight-filled gardens.

Kate sat on a tapestry-covered window seat, a glass of wine in her hand, the window open before her to the soft evening air, and dreamily she watched a swarm of mosquitoes that hovered over the lily pond in the gathering dusk. She wasn't too surprised when she was joined by Tom, but it did occur to her to wonder if it had only been her sister who had read the signs between them or whether anyone else had been as perceptive. It had also been her sister who had suggested that she was in love with Tom and he with her. Had she really fallen in love with him? Was he falling in love with her?

'You look lovely sitting there,' he murmured as he sat beside her, 'so cool and elegant and in control.'

She smiled up at him. 'I don't always feel in control these days,' she replied softly so that only they could hear.

'And why is that?' Tom raised his eyebrows in the quizzical way he had that she had come to recognise.

'I think it has something to do with someone who's swept into my life and turned it upside down.' Kate allowed her gaze to meet his, and her heart skipped a beat as she read the look in his eyes.

'Are you ready to go home yet?' he asked.

She nodded and stood up.

'Where's Nicola?' He looked around.

'She's staying the night.' Once more, briefly, she met his gaze.

'Your sister knew, didn't she?' asked Tom much later as they lay together in Kate's bed watching the pattern on the ceiling from the street lamp outside the window.

'She guessed something, yes,' admitted Kate, 'but then she is my sister and she knows me very well.'

'Is it that obvious?' queried Tom.

'She said she hasn't seen me looking this happy for a very long time.'

'And are you? Happy, I mean?'

'Yes, Tom, I am.'

'But how did she know it was me? We weren't together that much today.'

She hesitated, then shifted her position slightly so that her body fitted more comfortably against his. Their lovemaking had been even more passionate than before, with both of them reaching even greater depths of fulfilment, and she wondered if now was the right time to tell him about her initial attraction to him. His next question decided her.

'Maybe she didn't approve of me?' suggested Tom.

She took a deep breath. 'Tom, there's something I haven't told you.'

He had been gently stroking the contour of her hip beneath the thin sheet that covered them, but he stopped at her words and stared down at her.

'Go on,' he said quietly.

'It's nothing terrible,' she gave a nervous laugh, 'but I noticed it the moment I saw you.'

'Noticed what?' He frowned.

'That you're the image of Brian, my ex-husband.'

He was silent for a long moment, then he said, 'So is that what all this has been about?'

Kate stared up at his face but was unable to read

his expression in the half light. The tone of his voice, however, had hinted at what he was thinking.

'No, Tom. No,' she said quickly. 'That isn't it at all. It may have been what first attracted me to you, but. . .'

'You weren't simply trying to recapture something?'

'No. In fact, if that were the case the reverse would be true — I would have gone out of my way to avoid recapturing what I had with Brian.'

'It sounds as if your sister was concerned,' remarked Tom.

'Fran never liked Brian and I suppose she thought I might have fallen for the same type of man again, but I soon put her straight, I can assure you.'

'You mean you told her you hadn't fallen for me?'

'No, not that — that you're nothing whatsoever like Brian in your ways. You may look like him, but that's where it ends.'

'So does that mean you have fallen for me?' He moved his hand from her hips and gently cupped her breast.

She sighed and stretched. 'I don't know, Tom. I'm trying hard not to. After all, it isn't what we agreed, is it?'

'That's true,' he admitted. 'You said you didn't want any long-term commitment.'

'And you agreed. After all, you aren't going to be here for much longer, are you?'

'Right again, so if that's the case, what are we doing wasting precious time now?' He moved so that his body covered hers again, while she wound her arms around his neck burying her fingers in his thick hair, drawing his face down to hers and at the same time lifting her hips to meet his.

This time the urgency was gone, and they made love for hours, exploring each other's bodies and delighting in each other's reactions, and when finally they fell into exhausted sleep it was almost dawn.

When Kate next awoke sunlight flooded the room, and a glance at the bedside clock revealed that it was almost ten o'clock. Sounds from downstairs suggested that Tom was making tea, and this was confirmed when he appeared a few moments later with two steaming mugs.

'Well, good morning,' he said, smiling at her from the doorway.

Lazily she stretched, then when she saw he was wearing her towelling robe she smiled back. 'I had no idea it was so late. . . I ought to get up.'

'Drink your tea first,' he said, sitting on the edge of the bed. 'You must be tired—we didn't exactly get much sleep, did we?' His gaze met hers and she sighed, recalling the night they'd spent. Surprisingly she found that now she had slept she didn't feel tired, simply contented and at peace with the world.

They sipped their tea, taking their time and talking about the party and the people who had been there. The only warning of what was to follow was a slight sound from downstairs.

Tom raised his head. 'Nicola. . .?' Alarm flickered in his eyes.

Kate shook her head, but at the same time pulled the sheet over her breasts. 'No. . .she was going swimming with the others. She won't be back until lunchtime. . .it's probably only the Sunday papers. . .' It was all she had time to say before they heard a thumping sound on the stairs. Tom half rose to his feet, then the door suddenly opened and Nicola burst into the room.

'Mum, I want my cossie, you're not still in. . . bed. . .' She trailed off, her eyes widening in disbelief as she looked from Kate to Tom and then back to Tom again. 'Oh!' she gasped, her hand flying to her mouth.

For a moment no one spoke, then Kate and Tom began speaking together.

'Nicola——' Kate began.

'Hello, Nicky. . .' Tom tried to sound casual, but even in his voice there was a tinge of embarrassment.

Nicola continued to stare at them, then abruptly, without another word, she turned and stumbled from the room.

'Nicola. . .!' Kate called after her, and struggled up in the bed, pulling the sheet around her.

'Leave her,' said Tom quietly, putting a restraining hand on her arm.

'But I can't—I must explain. . .' Kate mumbled.

'Whatever you say would only make things worse.'

She sank back against her pillows with a sigh. This was the last thing she had wanted to happen.

They sat in silence and heard Nicola rummaging around in her bedroom, then she ran down the stairs, and moments later they heard the front door slam behind her.

Tom sighed and stood up. 'Well, she knows now,' he said, looking ruefully down at Kate. 'How do you think she'll take it?'

'You saw the look on her face. I imagine she'll be pretty upset—that's why I didn't want her to find out.'

'Would she have reacted in the same way if it had been anyone else, or is it just because it's me?' he asked.

'I'm not entirely sure—I don't make a habit of this, you know,' said Kate grimly, then with a sigh she added, 'But yes, it probably is because it's you. I told you, I think she has a crush on you.'

'I know that's what you said, but Nicola's only a——'

'Only a child?' interrupted Kate. 'Is that what you were going to say? Love hurts just as much at thirteen as it does at thirty, and this will hurt her doubly because it's me you're with. I told you, she already said that you were her friend and not mine.'

'Oh, God!' Tom shrugged helplessly and turned to the window. 'And now I've hurt her. I wouldn't have done that for the world, Kate, you know that. I've become very fond of Nicola.' He turned then and looked at Kate, and she saw the sincerity in his face. 'Would you like me to try and talk to her?'

She shook her head. 'No, thanks all the same, Tom, but I think that has to be my job.'

'Very well, but let me know if you need any help.'

His eyes narrowed suddenly as if he'd just thought of something. 'Does Nicola know I resemble her father?'

'I don't think so. I certainly haven't said anything,' said Kate.

'But hasn't she seen photographs of him?'

'There were a couple around when she was tiny, but she hasn't seen one recently. I must confess, though, that I did wonder if she felt drawn to you — you know, something in the genes — because you're so like her father, or maybe in her subconscious she does remember him.'

'And now all her illusions have been shattered.' Tom paused. 'And where does that leave us?'

'Leave her to me, Tom. I'll do my best to make her understand — she'll probably now see you as a threat to the life she and I have here. I'll have to make her see that it won't change anything, because what we have is only temporary.'

When he didn't answer Kate threw him a sharp glance, then said, 'Come on, we mustn't let it spoil what little time we have left.'

But it did spoil the rest of the day, and when, after Tom had left to take over the on-call from Malcolm and Nicola still hadn't returned, Kate began to get very edgy.

It was early evening when she finally heard her daughter's key in the door. 'You've been a long time,' she said as Nicola sauntered into the kitchen. It came out accusingly, something that Kate cer-

tainly hadn't intended, for she didn't want to antag-
onise Nicola any further.

'I didn't see any point in hurrying home,' retorted
Nicola as she fished her swimming gear out of her
bag and loaded it into the washing machine.

'Nicola. . .about what you saw. . .'

'I know what I saw,' said Nicola coolly, 'so don't
say it wasn't what I thought. That's what you were
going to say, wasn't it?' She arched her eyebrows in
a way so reminiscent of her father that Kate swallowed and looked away. 'You'd been to bed with
Tom — it's as simple as that. I don't suppose it was
the first time either. . .was it?'

Kate looked up quickly and saw the pain in her
daughter's eyes. 'Nicky, please let me explain. . .'

'Going on all the time, was it?' Suddenly Nicola
looked frighteningly adult. 'And there was me thinking Tom was my friend, that he came here to see
me, and all the time you and he. . .' Turning, she
ran from the kitchen, and Kate heard her footsteps
as they thudded up the stairs to her room, followed
by the slamming of her bedroom door.

Kate knew it would be useless to follow her, that
her daughter needed time to calm down, so it was a
good hour later when she made her way to Nicola's
room with two mugs of coffee and a packet of
chocolate digestive biscuits.

She found Nicola in her habitual position, on her
bed watching her television with her arms round her
pink hippo. Kate gave an inward smile; there was so
much of her daughter that was still child. Carefully

she set down the mugs and sat on the side of the bed and offered Nicola a biscuit. When she refused she took one herself and took a bite.

'Nicky, we have to talk about this,' she said.

'There's nothing to talk about.'

'I think there is. I know I deceived you, but it was with the best of intentions.'

'It generally is,' said Nicola with a wisdom far beyond her years, and Kate knew she was referring to how she had deceived her over visiting Kim's house.

'I knew you'd be hurt, I knew you looked on Tom as your friend, that's why I didn't tell you.'

'But you didn't stop, did you?'

'No,' admitted Kate, 'I didn't stop, because I happen to be very fond of Tom.'

'Even though you knew I was fond of him?'

'Nicky love, Tom can still be your friend, but he's far too old for you for anything else.'

'I wondered when you'd bring that into it,' muttered Nicola.

'What?'

'The age difference. But while we're on that subject, what about the difference between him and you?'

'What about it?' Kate tried to sound casual, but the doubt she herself had always had began to niggle again at the back of her mind.

'You're much too old for him,' said Nicola bluntly.

'Nicola. . .!'

'Well, you are. . .you know what my friends will

say when they find out. . .they'll say he's your toyboy!'

Kate stared at her, then angrily drew in her breath. 'Well, you won't have to worry about it for much longer,' she said tightly.

'What do you mean?' demanded Nicola.

'Ruth Scott will be back soon and Tom will be returning to the States—so neither of us will have him around.' Kate stood up and hurried from the room, the coffee and her half-eaten biscuit forgotten.

Kate spent a restless night with Nicola's words echoing in her brain. Was she really too old for Tom? He had never referred to the difference in their ages, but he must be aware of it. Her own common sense told her that she wasn't the first woman to fall for a younger man, neither would she be the last, and that in many cases it worked perfectly well even when there was a much greater difference. But was that how other people would see it? Her family? Her colleagues? Nicola's friends?

Angrily she tossed and turned, trying to dismiss such thoughts from her mind. What did it matter what other people thought? How often had she encouraged her clients to disregard what others thought, so why could she not now follow her own advice?

Surely all that mattered was how she and Tom felt, and if their lovemaking the previous night had been anything to go by there was little lacking in their relationship.

With that comforting thought uppermost in her mind she finally fell into a fitful sleep, only to be awakened just before the dawn chorus by the disquieting question, what did any of it matter? In a few short weeks her relationship with Tom would be over, and the difference in their ages would be as inconsequential as yesterday's newspaper.

At the very thought of life without Tom, Kate felt as if she wanted to die, and, clutching at her pillow, she curled herself protectively into the foetal position, as if by doing so she could shut out the rest of the world and the cruel reality of what would shortly happen. But that had been the bargain they had made—a no-strings affair—so at the end they could both walk away.

What, of course, she hadn't bargained for was that she might fall in love. And what of Tom? Fran had said it was obvious he was in love with her.

But was he, or was the reason the age difference didn't matter to him the fact that he knew it was only a short-term concern?

CHAPTER TEN

KATE found great difficulty in concentrating that morning, having too many problems of her own to be able to clear her mind sufficiently to be receptive to her clients' needs. Tom had already started an early surgery when she arrived at the centre, so she knew she wouldn't even see him until much later in the morning.

Fortunately her first client was Robert, the young man with the claustrophobia problem, and the therapy she had chosen for him seemed to be showing results. He seemed optimistic and full of hope that he would be able to make the planned trip to Europe with his girlfriend the following weekend. As he left her room at the end of his session Kate felt herself begin to unwind — only to be told by Julie a few minutes later that her client Stephanie had come into the centre in a dreadful state seeking an emergency appointment.

Kate saw her immediately, and found that the reason for her distress was that her new man, Gerry, had gone back to his wife. Kate allowed her to talk through her anguish, then managed to bring the conversation round to practical matters.

'Will you stay in the flat?' she asked gently when Stephanie paused to blow her nose.

'I can't. Gerry was paying the rent and I lost my job soon after I left Mike. I can't afford to stay at the flat — the rent's far too high.'

'Is there anyone you could stay with?'

Stephanie shook her head. 'There's my sister, but I don't think she'd have me there after what's happened — she isn't even speaking to me.'

Kate remained silent, and Stephanie looked up sharply. 'I'm not going back to Mike,' she insisted.

'I wasn't suggesting you should,' replied Kate. 'But you have to go somewhere. I think you should go and see your sister. . .'

'I can't! She won't. . .'

'She might, you know. She is your sister, after all, and sisters do have the habit of coming up trumps when you least expect it.'

When Stephanie still looked dubious Kate went on, 'Tell you what, try your sister first, then if she won't play ball I'll get on to Social Services for you and see if we can arrange temporary accommodation.'

'You mean one of those bed-and-breakfast places?'

'Just until you sort yourself out.'

Stephanie stared at her, then her eyes filled with tears again. 'I can't believe Gerry's gone back to her — he told me it was all over, that he didn't love her any more. They hadn't slept together for months — and it was so good between us — it really was. Maybe he'll come back. . .' she gulped.

'Maybe he will,' said Kate gently, 'but you have

to be prepared that he won't. Do what I've said, then get back to me. Even if you stay with your sister, I want to see you again tomorrow.'

After Stephanie had left, Kate had a demanding therapy session with her group with alcohol-related problems, and when she finally made her way to the staff-room at lunchtime she felt drained. The room was empty, and thankfully she poured herself some coffee and sat down, resting her head against the back of the chair.

She must have dozed for a few moments, for she was unaware of anyone coming into the room, and it was the touch of a hand on her arm that roused her. She opened her eyes and found Tom crouched down beside her. The loving look of concern on his face was almost her undoing.

'Oh, Tom!' she whispered, and heedless of anyone else who might come into the room, she rested her face against his.

His nearness seemed to make all the problems recede into the background, and for a moment she was perfectly content to remain quietly like that with him.

In the end it was he who moved first, drawing away from her slightly, then reaching out his hand and gently touching her cheek. 'Tough morning?' he asked softly.

She nodded, then said ruefully, 'After an even tougher night.'

'Nicola?'

'Something like that.'

'She took it badly, then?'

'Let's just say it wasn't easy making her understand.'

'Kate. . .' he hesitated 'I don't know how to say this, but would it be better—that is, would you rather we stopped seeing each other?'

She stared at him as if what he had suggested would be unthinkable, then her eyes clouded and she sighed. 'I know that would probably be the most sensible thing to do, but. . .is that what you want, Tom?'

'No, it isn't. I want to go on seeing you.'

'In spite of all the hassle?'

He grinned then. 'Yes, in spite of all the hassle.'

'That's what I want too,' she admitted.

'What about Nicola?'

'She'll just have to come to terms with it. . .' She broke off as Malcolm suddenly appeared in the doorway and stared at the two of them in amazement.

'Oh, I'm sorry, am I interrupting something?' he asked.

'No, come in, Malcolm.' Tom stood up.

'Actually it was Kate I wanted to see,' Malcolm went on, still with a slightly bemused expression on his face. 'I've persuaded Theo to come in, it's his lunch hour—I was wondering if you could see him now?'

Kate gave a barely audible sigh and stood up. 'Yes, all right, Malcolm, bring him up to my room in five minutes.'

As Malcolm left the staff-room she turned to Tom once more. 'That's given him something to think about,' she said with a tight little smile.

'I'm sorry, Kate, I don't want to make things awkward for you, whether it's with Nicola or here with the rest of the staff,' Tom told her.

'What you mean is that I'll be left to pick up the pieces after you've gone?'

'Something like that, yes.'

'Let me be the one to worry about that,' said Kate. 'Now, let me go and see if I can sort young Theo out.' She left Tom knowing he was still concerned about her, for although she had made light of picking up the pieces after he'd gone she knew it was going to be no easy task. He'd given her the choice to stop seeing him now, and she knew in her heart that that would probably have been the safer option, not only for Nicola's sake and the other problems their relationship presented, but also for her own sake.

Now she had recognised the fact that she was in love with Tom she knew any further time spent with him would only intensify her feelings and make the parting even more difficult. But she also knew that, faced with the choice, there was no way she could stop seeing him while she still had the chance.

Theo, a tall, handsome boy, with thick blond hair, bore little resemblance to his father, who was short and dark. He was polite to Kate, but he seemed unwilling to divulge any information as to what had induced him to take drugs.

In spite of her efforts to encourage him to open up and talk, he remained silent, only answering her questions in monosyllables. Then as the session was drawing to a close and Kate was thinking she had achieved nothing, she suggested he came for a further session to discuss his problem.

'Don't you mean my father's problem?' he said bluntly.

Kate looked at him quickly, but his expression remained impassive. 'You don't think you have a problem, Theo?'

'No.'

'You don't see the need to smoke pot as a problem?'

'Of course not.'

'Did you do it for a dare?'

He didn't answer, and Kate went on quickly, 'Or was it simply because it was there and everyone else was doing it?' Still he didn't answer, but his attitude seemed less hostile now. 'I understand this incident took place in a house in Cromwell Road?'

His grey eyes flickered as she mentioned Cromwell Road, then he nodded. 'A guy from school lives there — a few of us used to meet at his house.'

He fell silent again, and Kate got the impression that he decided he'd said enough.

After he had left she told Malcolm that she thought he didn't have much to worry about. 'I'm pretty certain it was a one-off. I don't think for one moment that Theo has the type of problems you're worried about.'

'I only hope you're right,' he said grimly. 'That lot in Cromwell Road are a weird bunch. Some of them seem to be living in some sort of commune.'

'Well, I should imagine the police have their eyes on the place now that drugs have been found there,' said Kate. Inwardly she was relieved that Nicola hadn't mentioned Kim again; at least that seemed to have blown over.

And for all that week Nicola didn't seem inclined to mention very much at all. When she was at home she kept mainly to her room, but most of her free time she seemed to be spending at Bev's house. Kate openly invited Tom to the house on several occasions, and while Nicola was coolly polite, there was a faintly contemptuous air about her, that on the one hand made Kate want to shake her and on the other made her long for the days when she and her daughter had got on so well together.

At work Kate continued her sessions with Stephanie, who had gone to stay with her sister, and who had had a visit from Mike, her husband. She was still adamant that she didn't want to go back to him, but at least they were now talking, and she seemed happier for seeing her children again.

Robert, the claustrophobic, had gone on his trip to France, and Kate awaited the outcome of that particular exercise, while Lottie had received an appointment for her X-ray. As she had promised,

Kate took her to the hospital and tried to calm her down as they waited, by talking of other things.

'Dr Beresford is taking Nicola and me to see some motor racing the weekend after next,' she said.

Lottie pulled a face. 'Dangerous stuff, that is; you wouldn't catch me going to one of them places.'

'Apparently it's very exciting, or so Dr Beresford tells me,' said Kate.

'Didn't he used to race himself?'

'Yes, he did.' Kate looked surprised, wondering how Lottie knew.

'Nicola told me.'

'Oh.' She fell silent, wondering what else Nicola had told Lottie about Tom. She threw her a sideways glance, but Lottie seemed much more concerned with what was going to happen to her in the next few minutes than in any gossip she might have heard concerning her employer and the locum GP.

At that moment the receptionist called Lottie into the X-ray unit and Kate was left alone. Idly she flicked through a pile of dog-eared magazines, at the same time thinking that Lottie probably didn't know anything and that she was just overreacting.

When Lottie emerged from the X-ray unit Kate looked up quickly. 'That wasn't too bad, was it?' She stood up, replacing the magazines on a low table.

''Tweren't no picnic,' muttered Lottie, pulling a face.

She was silent on the drive home, and it wasn't until Kate brought the car to a halt outside the neat brick semi-detached where Lottie lived that the older woman glanced at her and said, 'You and the doctor going together now, then?'

Kate only hesitated fractionally, instinct telling her it would be impossible to pull the wool over Lottie's eyes. 'Yes, Dr Beresford and I have been seeing each other,' she admitted, wondering what Lottie would make of the fact.

'Good for you — 'bout time you had a man in your life again.'

'He's a good bit younger than me, Lottie,' Kate heard herself say.

'Is he?' Lottie frowned. 'I hadn't realised. I just thought how happy you both looked when I came in yesterday. Besides, what's it matter if he is younger? Men have been doing it for years. . .going about with young girls. It's our turn now.' She turned and winked at Kate as she climbed from the car. 'You enjoy yourself, life's too short to worry about things like that. . . I wish it was me, and that's a fact. That Dr Beresford's a real dish!'

Kate was still chuckling when she arrived back at the centre, but her chat with Lottie had done her good, and she made up her mind that from that moment on she would simply enjoy the time that she and Tom had left, stop worrying about the difference in their ages, and about what Nicola thought.

She even made up her mind to stop thinking about the fact that very soon Tom would be leaving.

It was in this new positive frame of mind that she made plans for the weekend, arranging for Nicola to go to Fran's so that she could spend two whole days with Tom.

The weekend proved to be glorious, and it was only afterwards that Kate recognised it to be the calm before the storm. On Saturday evening they went back to the jazz club on the *Medina Queen*, then spent the night in each other's arms. On Sunday morning Tom repaired a fault on Kate's car while she cooked lunch for them both, then, after they had eaten, Tom drove her over to her sister's to collect Nicola.

Nicola, although quiet, seemed to have enjoyed her weekend, and by the time they all got back to the house for tea Kate was beginning to think that her daughter had accepted the situation between herself and Tom.

The week started well, with Robert reporting to Kate that his trip to France had been a success, then the first little cloud appeared on the horizon when Bernard announced that Ruth Scott would be returning to work the following week. 'I'm pleased she's recovered,' he said in the staff-room at lunchtime, 'but we shall all miss you, Tom.'

If only you knew how much! thought Kate as she looked across the room at Tom. The thought of life without him was now unbearable.

'When is it exactly you go back to the States?' Bernard asked, and Kate found herself holding her breath as she waited for Tom to answer the question she had refused to even contemplate asking.

'Almost immediately.' he said quietly, and his

gaze sought and briefly held Kate's. 'There are a lot of arrangements to be made over this proposed partnership, and I need to go out to Philadelphia as soon as I can book a flight.'

Kate tried to put it out of her mind, and then early on Tuesday afternoon a blow fell that was to make her temporarily forget everything else.

She had just finished a session with a man suffering from stress related to his job when her intercom sounded and Julie told her that a Mr Phillips, the manager of Sandells, one of the department stores in the precinct, was on the phone wanting to speak to her.

'Hello, Mr Phillips, this is Kate Riley. How can I help you?'

'Mrs Riley? I was wondering if you could come down to Sandells to see me.'

'What is it in connection with, Mr Phillips?' asked Kate, thinking that he might be a prospective client. His next words, however, put all such thoughts from her mind.

'You have a daughter, Nicola Riley?'

Kate's heart skipped a beat and her immediate thought was that Nicola had had another accident. 'I do. What's wrong, Mr Phillips?'

'Well, it's rather a delicate matter ——'

'Please, tell me,' Kate interrupted, 'what is it?'

'Very well, Mrs Riley. I'm afraid your daughter has been caught shoplifting by our detective.'

'*What*?' Kate was aghast, then she said, 'I think there must be some mistake. Nicola wouldn't. . .'

'It's the store's policy to prosecute shoplifters, Mrs Riley. We haven't, however, yet called the police, so if you would like to come down first.'

'I'll be there right away.' She replaced the receiver and found her hand was shaking. Nicola, shoplifting? It was impossible.

Stopping only to grab her bag and keys, she ran from her room, and collided with Tom in the corridor.

'Kate! Whatever's the hurry——?' Laughing, he took hold of her shoulders, then as he held her at arm's length and saw her expression, his smile disappeared. 'What's happened?'

She took a deep breath. 'It's Nicola, Tom. She's been caught shoplifting.'

'You're joking!' He said it in such a way that shoplifting would have been the very last thing he could have imagined Nicola doing.

'I wish I was,' said Kate. 'But I've just had the manager of Sandells on the phone, and he suggested I might like to go down there before they phone the police.'

'I'll come with you,' said Tom without any hesitation.

Thankfully she followed him to his car, happy to let him drive and to have him beside her to give moral support.

And later in the manager's office, where they found a silent, white-faced Nicola, it was Tom who took over and did the talking. On the drive to the store Kate had had dreadful visions of her daughter being caught with her pockets bulging with jewellery or cassettes or even make-up, and when it transpired that what she had taken was a packet of safety pins she had to fight a wave of hysterical relief.

'What she took is of little consequence,' said the manager sternly when Kate was unable to conceal her relief. 'It's the intent to steal that we're concerned with.'

'But my daughter isn't a thief,' protested Kate. 'Besides, what would she want with a packet of safety pins?'

'I've no idea, Mrs Riley, but we find it's very often the case that shoplifters take items they don't want or need.'

Kate fell silent, knowing from her own training that what he said was true—that in many cases the act itself was a cry for help. She glanced at Nicola, who hadn't spoken a word and was looking at the ground. Had she failed her daughter so much that she had driven her to this? Vaguely she became aware that Mr Phillips was going on about how much the store lost each year as a result of theft, and that was why it was their policy to prosecute, then Tom stepped in, and in the end it was he who persuaded the manager not to call the police, after convincing him that Nicola would receive the help she clearly needed.

They drove home in silence, and Tom had left them at the house and returned to the centre, but Nicola remained withdrawn and uncooperative, and no amount of questioning or reasoning on Kate's part would induce her to divulge why she had done it.

The week seemed to go from bad to worse when on Thursday morning Tom called Kate into his consulting-room and shut the door behind him.

'Any joy with Nicola?' he asked, and the concern in his voice as he anxiously scanned her features was only too apparent.

She shook her head. 'No, nothing, but I spoke to her teacher this morning and it appears she's been dodging school on several occasions. Oh, Tom, I wish I knew what it was all about! You don't think this is all the result of her. . .of her finding us together, do you? It isn't her way of retaliating?'

Tom shook his head. 'I don't think so, Kate. That may have something to do with it, but I think there's more here than meets the eye. Hasn't she said anything at all?'

'No, she refuses to discuss it with me.'

He thoughtfully walked to the window, then turning said, 'Do you think she might talk to me?'

'She might—I don't know. But you're certainly welcome to try.'

'I'll go and see her later,' he said, then leaning across his desk he picked up a piece of paper. 'I'm sorry, Kate, I'm afraid that isn't all.'

She looked at him fearfully, wondering what she was about to hear next.

'You know the old saying about troubles coming in battalions? Well, I'm afraid I have Lottie's X-ray result here.'

She stared at him, suddenly unable to speak.

He cleared his throat. 'It isn't good, Kate—the radiologist reports a neoplasm in the colon. I shall be referring her immediately to a surgeon.'

'Oh no—poor Lottie!' Kate sank down on to a chair.

'She'll be needing all the support she can get,' said Tom.

'Of course.' Kate made an attempt to pull herself together. 'I'll do all I can for her. Lottie has been very good to me in the past; this will be my way of doing something for her.' She looked up as someone knocked on the door, then as Tom called out Julie popped her head round.

'Oh, Kate, there you are,' she said. 'Theo Symonds is in Reception, he's asking to see you.'

Theo's attitude seemed to have changed drastically from the last time Kate had seen him, and as he sat down in her consulting-room Kate imagined he had come to talk about his problems. She was startled therefore when he began by saying, 'I've heard that Nicola's in trouble, Mrs Riley.'

Her eyes narrowed, then she remembered that in the past when the partners had held family parties and she and Nicola had been included, Nicola and Theo had always appeared to get on well together.

'What have you heard, Theo?' she asked.

'Someone at school said she'd been caught shoplifting.'

'That's right, she was,' agreed Kate.

'Has she talked about it?' Theo looked uncomfortable now and shifted in his chair.

'If you mean has she offered any explanation as to why she did it, then the answer is no. Do you know anything about it, Theo?' She looked at him intently, but he avoided her gaze. 'What I can't understand is why she should risk everything for a packet of safety pins——'

'That was the whole point, to take something worthless. . .' he said quickly, then lapsed into silence.

Kate took a deep breath. 'Theo, I think you know what this is all about. Would you please care to explain?'

CHAPTER ELEVEN

'WOULD you believe it was part of an initiation ceremony?'

'What!' Tom stared at Kate across his desk.

'I've just had Theo Symonds in to see me. He wasn't prepared to talk before, but when he heard Nicola was in trouble he decided it was time he spoke up.'

As Tom indicated a chair Kate thankfully sat down; she was still feeling a little stunned from what Theo had told her, and she needed to talk.

'Apparently the group Theo was caught with for smoking pot used to meet in the basement of a house in Cromwell Road.'

'Go on.' Tom's eyes had narrowed at the mention of Cromwell Road.

'The boy who lived at the house was called Crispin. He's Kim's brother. They'd formed themselves into a group and called themselves the Hell Fire Club.'

Tom raised his eyebrows, and Kate nodded. 'Yes, and it sounds as if it could have been every bit as notorious as the old Hell Fire Club of the past if it had been given the chance. According to Theo, prospective members had to pass a series of tests before being accepted. Pot-smoking was just one of them; the others were unmentionable.' She shuddered.

'Are you telling me Nicola was involved in this?' Tom stared at her.

'Not quite.' Kate drew a deep breath before continuing. 'Apparently Kim, annoyed at not being able to join the all-male domain of her brother's club, formed one of her own — the rules were similar and the initiations included stealing some small item from a different shop in the precinct every day for a week, playing truant from school, drinking spirits, smoking pot and, would you believe, sleeping with a boy from the Hell Fire Club?'

'Good God!' For a moment Tom seemed lost for words, then leaning back in his chair, he said, 'Do you know exactly just how much Nicola did?'

'No, but I certainly mean to find out,' said Kate grimly.

'Kate, just a minute.' Tom stood up and came round the desk, standing before her and taking her by the shoulders. 'Will you still let me talk to her?'

'I don't know.' Kate hesitated.

'You were happy to let me try before.'

'Yes, I know, but that was before I found out all this — honestly, Tom, I had no idea it was so serious. There was something about that girl Kim that I didn't trust, but I didn't for one moment imagine that she and her brother were involved in such things.'

'I hope someone's doing something to put a stop to it.'

Kate nodded. 'Theo and Malcolm have gone to the headmaster, it'll be up to him to take any further steps he considers necessary. But that won't solve my problem with Nicola. Honestly, Tom, I call myself a counsellor, but when it comes to my own daughter I don't know where to start.'

'As I said before, it's different when it's your own, you're too close to it — that's why I'd like you to let me try.'

'You — counselling?' She allowed herself a faint smile at the prospect.

'Why not? Besides, it would be nice to try and sort things out before our trip to Silversmead on Saturday.'

'Nicola said she didn't want to go last night,' said Kate gloomily.

'That's all the more reason for me to try and break through the barriers she's put up and remind her that she really does want to go.' As he spoke Tom looked down at Kate, then drew her gently into his arms.

With a sigh she leaned against him, comforted by his nearness and suddenly content that he should want to deal with her problems.

'Do you think, Tom,' she asked after a few moments, 'that all this is a direct result of our relationship? That Nicola felt so betrayed that it was her way of retaliating?'

'It may have been her initial reaction, but it sounds as if it was all getting out of control. Thank God Theo had the sense to come forward!'

Kate nodded. 'He and Nicola have always been fond of one another. He told me that he couldn't bear the thought of Nicola being mixed up in that group.'

'Just as I can't bear the thought of you being miserable.' Tom kissed the tip of her nose. 'So I want you to leave things to me.' Then, oblivious to anyone who might come into his room, he drew her closer, his mouth covering hers in a kiss that thrilled her and left her yearning for more.

Saturday was one of those days where the heat shimmered above the road and the tar blistered and burst beneath the wheels of Tom's BMW. Kate sat in the back of the car and watched Nicola, who sat in the passenger seat beside Tom. She didn't know what had been said between Tom and her daughter during the two hours they had spent together; she only knew that Nicola, although still subdued, seemed in a much better frame of mind than she had previously been. She even seemed to be enjoying the prospect of the day ahead, and Kate found herself relaxing, knowing that she would have been totally happy if it hadn't been for the prospect of Tom's imminent departure.

They travelled for about fifty miles along the M3 motorway, then turned off at the junction marked for Silversmead. The huge track, home of Formula One motor racing, was a further five miles, and as they drove in through the main entrance and an official directed them to the car parking areas, Kate sensed an excitement about Tom as he began explaining things to Nicola.

'Today is the first day of the Grand Prix,' he said as he parked the car. 'This morning will be taken up with practice runs and the real race will begin after lunch. I thought perhaps you'd like to look round the stalls first—there's always plenty to buy. After we've had lunch I have tickets for us for the main grandstand on the straight.'

As they stepped from the car the first thing that struck Kate was the noise from the practising cars. When he saw her expression, Tom laughed. 'This is nothing—wait until the real thing starts, you won't be able to hear yourself think!'

Tom's excitement seemed to transmit itself to Nicola, and as Kate watched her hopping up and down and darting from one trade stand to the next she felt a wave of relief that there was now no sign of the moody, rebellious teenager of the past few weeks.

After browsing round the stalls they walked part way round the track and sat on the grass to watch some of the practice runs. Tom took the trouble to explain much of what was happening, and even Kate found herself listening with interest as Tom's enthusiasm and extensive knowledge of the sport became more and more obvious.

Then while Tom went off in search of soft drinks for them all Nicola turned excitedly to Kate. 'This is absolutely brilliant—I told you motor racing was exciting, didn't I?' she demanded.

'Yes, you did,' agreed Kate.

'Are you all right?' Nicola peered back at Kate.

'Yes, why?'

'I don't know, you look a bit off.'

'Thanks! I expect it's the heat, that's all. And I am a bit tired; I haven't been sleeping that well,' said Kate.

Nicola didn't answer immediately, keeping her eyes to the front as if she was concentrating on the practice run that was going on, then without turning round, she said. 'You mean because of me, don't you?'

'What do you mean?'

'That's why you haven't been sleeping—because of me?' Nicola turned then and looked at her mother.

Kate shrugged. 'That's partly the reason, I suppose.'

'And the other part is because Tom's going away, isn't it?'

The directness of the question caught Kate unawares, and she drew in her breath sharply, then she sighed, letting her breath go. 'Yes, I suppose so,' she said quietly.

'You love him, don't you, Mum?' Nicola had plucked a piece of grass and was nonchalantly chewing the stem.

Kate was silent for a moment and the only sound was the distant roar of the cars as they negotiated some far area of the track and the closer humming of a bee as it hovered over a clump of clover, then quietly she said, 'Yes, Nicky, I love him.'

'He's great, isn't he?'

'How do you mean?' Suddenly Kate was curious as to how Tom had handled Nicky's problems.

'He didn't get mad at me at all. We just talked. . . Mum?'

'Yes, Nicky?'

'I'm sorry. I didn't know I'd upset you so much. . . I didn't mean to—you know. . .well, I might have done at first, I was angry, you see, about you and Tom. I thought Tom was my friend and I thought you'd pinched him from me. I went back to seeing Kim to get my own back because I knew you didn't like her. Then it all went horribly wrong. . .it was awful, the things she said I had to do. . .but by then I didn't know how to get out of it.'

'What was it about Kim that attracted you in the first place, Nicola?' asked Kate gently.

'I'm not sure,' Nicola answered slowly, then, reflecting, she went on, 'She was so different, I suppose, and I think it was something about how they all lived together at that house in Cromwell Road. There were so many of them, they seemed like one huge family, and—well, at home there are just us two, aren't there.'

That's what she's missed out on, thought Kate as Tom suddenly appeared bearing cans of Coke. I've tried to be mother and father to her, but she's missed being part of a family, not knowing what it is to have a father or brothers and sisters.

Later Tom took them for lunch in the hospitality tent of a well-known tyre manufacturer. Kate realised that this had been previously arranged, as several of the officials seemed to know Tom, and she found herself wondering just how great his own involvement in the racing scene had been.

The highlight of the day came after lunch when they took their grandstand seats, and, as the cars roared and jostled and finally accelerated away in clouds of heat and dust on the first lap of the Grand Prix, Kate understood what Tom had meant by the noise level. It was deafening; and it seemed that, just when her eardrums were recovering from the first onslaught, the cars were back on the second lap. Gradually, as one lap followed another, Kate felt she was becoming mesmerised, not only by the unbelievable noise but by the heat that shimmered above the track, giving a distorted image of the cars as sun glinted on metal, and by the pungent smell from the pits, one of burning rubber and high-octane fuel.

Eventually, when Tom suggested taking Nicola round to the pits, Kate was glad to escape from the grandstand and find a spot on the grass in the shade of a clump of sycamore trees.

As she watched them walk away she was struck again by how good Tom was with Nicola. He seemed to hit on just the right approach, and Kate found herself wondering what Brian would have been like with his daughter if the marriage had lasted.

She leaned back and closed her eyes, content to

drift for a while and leave Nicola to Tom. Suddenly she felt very weary, as if for the past few weeks she had been fighting some uphill battle. The roar of the cars as they negotiated the track formed a background drone to her thoughts, and in her spot in the shade out of the glare and intense heat of the sun Kate dozed for a while.

She was awakened by the sound of Nicola's excited chatter. She opened her eyes and found the pair of them looking down at her.

'Oh, Mum, surely you haven't been asleep! How could you, when all this is going on!' Nicola waved towards the continuing din from the cars in their seemingly never-ending circuit of the track.

Kate smiled and her gaze met Tom's. She was immediately struck by the concern in his eyes, and she thought how nice it was for a man to care about her, even if it was only to be for a short period of time.

'I met two of the drivers.' Nicola was bubbling with excitement. 'Just wait till I tell Theo. . .he'll be green with envy!'

'They were two of the guys I used to know in my own racing days,' Tom explained with a grin.

'Did you do much racing?' asked Kate curiously, wondering how he'd found the time.

'A bit. But it was only a hobby, I didn't race professionally.'

'Tom had a friend who won the British Grand Prix, didn't you, Tom,' Nicola turned excitedly to him. 'It was him who got Tom interested,' she explained to Kate.

As she was speaking Kate saw some emotion flit across Tom's features, and knowing him as well as she now did encouraged her to say, 'What happened to your friend, Tom?'

'He was badly burned in an accident at Le Mans,' he told her quietly.

Kate shuddered. 'Is that when you gave it up?'

He shrugged. 'More or less, I suppose. I decided I owed it to my patients to stay alive and put my training into practice.'

'I've always thought it must be the most dangerous sport around,' she said quietly.

'That's not necessarily true, in fact there are very few accidents on the track these days — you run more risk on the roads than in a racing car,' Tom told her.

'That may be so, but I'm glad I'm not watching you race.'

Their eyes met and his look clearly expressed his pleasure that she cared so much about him.

'Well, if Theo becomes a Formula One driver, I shall watch him in every race,' announced Nicola, then moving away from them towards the barriers, she glanced over her shoulder and added, 'That's if I don't become a driver myself. . .and I just might.'

'Oh, my God!' groaned Kate, rolling her eyes. 'What have you started, Tom Beresford?'

He threw his head back and laughed, and as the sun caught his wheat-coloured hair she thought he had never looked more handsome. 'There was me thinking you'd sorted out my daughter's problems when in fact you seem to have generated a whole new batch!'

'She's a lovely girl, your daughter,' he said, putting out his hand and helping Kate to her feet. 'But she's headstrong, and if you thought you had problems with her choice of girlfriends, you just wait and see now that she's into boyfriends.'

She glanced sharply at him. 'You mean Theo? But they've been friends since they were children.'

'But Kate, they aren't children any more, are they?'

She sighed. 'No, I suppose they aren't. I guess I should be grateful it's Theo and not that Crispin or whatever his name was.'

Tom glanced at his watch, 'We'd better be thinking about moving,' he said reluctantly, 'I'm doing the late on-call.'

Half an hour later they were heading home down the motorway. This time Kate sat beside Tom while Nicola sat in the back of the car and sorted out the car sticker, key-ring and the T-shirt that Tom had bought her, and her precious programme that had been signed by two of the drivers.

It was still very humid, as if a storm was brewing, the heat still quivered above the tarmac and a bank of indigo cloud had formed on the horizon. As other cars zipped past them carrying families returning home from their various weekend activities, Kate allowed herself to imagine briefly that they were like any other family — that she and Tom were married, that Nicola was their daughter and there was no threat of an imminent parting.

And it was then, as she indulged in that brief spell of fantasy, that a van in the line of traffic ahead suddenly burst a tyre and spun out of control, hitting the central reservation.

The next few seconds to Kate were as if she was seeing them in slow motion; with a terrific impact a car in front of them crashed into the van, while several other cars slewed across the motorway as the drivers fought to control them. Tom braked and managed to draw to the hard shoulder, bringing the car to a halt.

There followed a moment of utter silence, an eerie, unreal moment where even the cars hurtling by on the opposite side of the motorway seemed to belong to another world. For a split second they remained still, shocked, mesmerised by the heap of twisted metal on the road ahead, then like puppets they jerked alive again. Nicola gave a sound like a choking gasp, and Kate turned instinctively to see that she was all right.

Tom set the hazard lights going, then thrust his car phone into Kate's hands. 'Ring for the emergency services,' he said, then he leapt from the car and pulled his case from the boot.

Kate dialled the emergency number and asked for the police and ambulance after giving her name and location on the motorway, then scrambling from the car she looked back at her daughter, who was sitting wide-eyed and shocked on the back seat.